# Murder in
# C Major

# Murder in
# C Major

Sara Hoskinson Frommer

Poisoned Pen Press

Copyright © 1986 by Sara Hoskinson Frommer

First Trade Paperback Edition 2000

10 9 8 7 6 5 4 3 2 1

Library of Congress Catalog Card Number: 99-06872

ISBN: 1-890208-31-0

Poisoned Pen Press
6962 E. First Ave. Ste 103
Scottsdale, AZ 85251
www.poisonedpenpress.com
sales@poisonedpenpress.com

Printed in the United States of America

*With special thanks to Gabe,
to Marcia, and to Captain Charles Brown
of the Bloomington Police Department*

For Fritz Jauch
1921-1983
and to honor my father and mother

# Chapter One

Ironing for a corpse wasn't Joan Spencer's idea of fun. She hitched up her jeans, tested the iron's sizzle with two wet fingers, and creased the first shirt she touched.

Coming back to live in Oliver should have felt like old home week, but it was turning into pure murder. And something didn't make sense. Ignoring the crease as she jabbed the iron's point fiercely between the buttons, she thought back to that first orchestra rehearsal—had it really been less than two weeks ago?

♮♮♮

Joan rested her viola case on the gravel in the dark parking lot and searched the shadows for a way in. The sprawling new Alcorn County Consolidated School dwarfed the limestone Oliver School building she remembered from so many years earlier.

"Thank heaven for small mercies—there's a bass."

Some twenty feet away, a minuscule Toyota was being delivered of a string bass and a long-legged stool by a short, round man who had to be going her way. Joan picked up her instrument and concentrated on catching up with him before he reached his destination.

She made it in time to open the suddenly obvious door for him. Encumbered by an instrument bigger than he was and pointing the stool awkwardly ahead, the little man nodded his thanks and struggled down a long corridor without a word.

She followed, bothered by her sudden shyness. All I have to do is introduce myself, she thought, but she couldn't make the words come.

Her fingertips felt too cold to play.

Suddenly the little bass player stormed a door with the legs of his stool and Joan was enveloped in the cacophony of an orchestra warming up. The bassist was already lugging his burdens up some side steps to the stage of the small auditorium. Balancing her case across two armrests, Joan added it to the others already littering the empty seats. She took out her viola, stretched the shoulder rest across the back, tightened the bow, and gave it a few quick swipes with the rosin. It couldn't need much, as little as she had been playing.

She climbed to the stage and paused, uncertain whether to find a seat or speak to the conductor first. But he didn't seem to have arrived yet. Most of the orchestra was seated, although a string of violinists stood laughing and talking along one side. The first stand of violas had its complement of players. At the second, a balding man with a cheerful face sat alone.

"May I sit here? I don't know how you do things."

"Sure, happy to have you. There are never enough of us."

Joan settled into fourth chair in time to see the concert-master gesture to the first oboe for an A. She was grateful to discover that this orchestra tuned winds and strings separately, and not a bit surprised when the winds started noodling again before she'd brought her recalcitrant C string under control. Some things, she thought wearily, are the same everywhere.

She realized why she hadn't found the conductor when a woman—about five feet tall, round, and ruddy-faced—hefted herself onto the podium, laid a score on the stand, and picked up the baton. Alex Campbell was her name, Joan knew from the publicity she'd seen about this first rehearsal of the Oliver Civic Symphony season. It hadn't occurred to her that Alex was one of those names.

"Welcome back, everyone," Alex was saying, "and a special welcome to the new people. It looks as if we'll need to schedule some auditions. I'd like to hear all new winds during the coming week. For tonight, please double parts. I prefer to mix strong players all through the string section, but if you care where you sit, sign up for an audition. Yoichi Nakamura, our manager, has the sign-up sheets. Yoichi, do you want to say anything?"

A young Japanese man stood, violin in hand, among the seconds. His eyes danced, and his pointy smile reminded Joan of the delightful *haniwa* figures she had seen only in pictures. When he spoke, his barely discernible accent marked him as foreign born.

"Thank you. Please remember to fill out the registration cards on your stands. Write your name as you want it to appear on the concert program. I will have the sign-up sheets for auditions at the door for you. Also the sign-out sheets for borrowing music. That is very important. We must know where to find the music, especially after a concert. We paid two hundred dollars for missing rental parts last year. Next week I will bring you a personnel list and the rehearsal and concert schedules for the whole year. Thank you very much."

He didn't quite bow as he sat down, but Joan thought his quick look at his chair was not altogether to see if it was still there. She wondered whether he was one of the Suzuki-trained violinists now beginning to pepper American orchestras.

"Are we tuned? Yes?" asked Alex. "Then we'll begin with the Schubert."

The Schubert turned out to be the Great C Major Symphony. They read straight through the first three movements, interrupting only when a whole section of players was hopelessly lost. The beginning wobbled as September beginnings do among musicians who spend more of their summer in swimming pools than in practice rooms. But when the oboe solo danced over the violas' pom-pom-pom-pom at the beginning of the second movement, Joan began to rejoice. By intermission she was very glad she had screwed up the courage to come.

Her stand partner introduced himself as John Hocking, an engineer for one of the two electronics firms in Oliver. His daughter, he said, was over in the back of the second fiddles.

"I'm Joan Spencer. I've just come back to Indiana, but I lived here a long time ago. In fact, I've been wondering if I might know anybody in the orchestra."

"You might. Some of these folks go back as far as you possibly could. Don't let me keep you. I'm a recent arrival, myself. Over there by the punch and cookies you could run into almost anyone."

"I wonder if I'd recognize anybody after all this time," she said, getting up. "Can I bring you anything?"

"Thanks, but I'm trying to pretend I don't want any."

Joan grinned and laid her loosened bow on the stand. With the viola tucked under her arm, she threaded her way between cello stands to a table in the wings of the stage behind the basses. There she accepted a Styrofoam cup and a cookie from a woman whose tailored elegance and coiffure called for formal afternoon tea. Looking ruefully at her own scuffed sneakers, Joan wished she had a free hand to tuck up the hair she felt straggling down her neck.

The only good thing to be said for the nondescript fruit drink was that it was wet and cold. Could she have been shivering only an hour ago? But that had been jitters. An hour's vigorous playing had warmed her from fingertips to sodden underarms.

The cookie, homemade and lacy around the edges, proclaimed at least one sheep among the goats of the refreshment committee.

All around her, old friends were greeting each other. Except for the horns, who were taking advantage of the break to work on a chorale that nibbled at the edges of her memory, and the inevitable trumpet showing off his triple tonguing, the players seemed thoroughly jumbled. Many had left their instruments behind. Only a few of the fiddle players bore the rough, red brand of the chin rest beneath their jaws, battle scar of long hours of practice. Some were too young to have achieved one, but more, she suspected, were amateurs like her, who played for pleasure and stopped short of pain.

Paying the teenagers scant attention, Joan concentrated on people her age or older. No one looked familiar. Hardly surprising, after almost thirty years, but a disappointment nonetheless.

To her annoyance, the shyness had come creeping back. An inner voice needled, You don't belong here. You'll never feel at home again. With a now-or-never feeling, she introduced herself to a white-haired man standing alone.

"Hello. I'm Joan Spencer and I'm new."

"Elmer Rush. So am I."

"New to Oliver, or just the orchestra?"

"Both. My daughter and her family moved here this summer. Then her husband died, and I came to be with her and the children."

Joan blinked. "I'm sure that's a help."

"She makes me feel welcome. And one of the children needs a lot of special care."

She smiled. "Mine didn't, but at times during the past few years I would have sold my soul for someone to help me yell at them."

Elmer nodded. "How old are they now?"

"Pretty well grown. My daughter's on her own, with her first real job, and my son's in high school."

"You're still busy, then."

"Oh, I don't know. Actually, I don't see that much of Andrew. Not that I'd want him in my lap all the time. Generally, I'm glad he's so independent."

They moved back into the orchestra. Elmer crossed behind her to the bassoon section. He would have to audition later in the week, Joan remembered. She wished him luck.

Just as she reached her seat, she felt a hand on her shoulder.

"Joan Zimmerman! Is that really you? What are you doing here?"

It took her a moment to recognize in the rounded features of the tall woman beside her a member of Miss Duffy's sixth-grade class. Then it was easy. Nancy Krebs was now a dead ringer for her own mother.

"Nancy! I wondered what happened to you, but I didn't know how to find out."

"I almost didn't speak. I hardly knew you without your chipmunk cheeks. My dear, you have bones! You must tell me how you do it. Your hair's darker than I remembered, too—or do you help it a little? Skinned back like that, it reminds me of when you wore pigtails. Remember?"

Joan remembered efficient fingers catching every last strand of her hair in french braids so tight they stretched the corners of her eyes. Her own sloppy twist was skewered at the top with a wooden pin and felt in imminent danger of coming undone. She chuckled at the thought of working to cover the occasional gray strands she'd been seeing recently. It was fun, though, that Nancy noticed how streamlined she was these days.

"I always expected to see you at a class reunion," Nancy rattled on.

"Why? The high school never knew me."

"Never mind, You're here now. Look we've got to catch up on each other. I'd offer you a ride home tonight if I hadn't ridden with another trombone player."

"Nancy, I can drive if you'll tell me where to go. I'd love to talk. You can't believe how good it feels to see someone I know."

"Great. I'll find you after rehearsal." She scuttled back to the trombones. The conductor was already tapping for order.

Joan's stand partner was grinning. "Looks as if you know the one person in this bunch who can tell you more about what goes on in Oliver than the rest of us put together—and I bet she will."

Joan thought back. Even at twelve, Nancy Krebs had known everyone else's business. I wonder if I've changed as little as that, she mused.

The rest of the rehearsal dragged. Partly it was because she was eager for the kind of conversation she'd expected ever since arriving in Oliver a month earlier, but partly it was because Alex Campbell apparently thought half a rehearsal was enough for warming up to the music. In this half, she was beginning to work on it, often with individual sections. She began with the long-short-longs of the first movement. The concertmaster and principal second violin debated separate bows and hooking, and Alex concentrated on exact eighth notes, rather than the triplets into which they tended to slide. Then she and the violins attacked the written triplets that rose into the stratosphere at the end of the Andante section.

Looking around, Joan realized that this must be the pattern of Alex's rehearsals. Other people were prepared for it. Several players had books in their laps. A couple of students were bent over homework. The oboists to her right were making new reeds—or were they improving the ones they had? A visibly pregnant cellist was furrowing her brow over intricate knitting. John Hocking had borrowed the music from the first stand of violas to pencil in their bowings.

Unoccupied, Joan found it hard to keep from dozing off. In spite of the long wait, however, or maybe because it gave her a chance to listen, she found her admiration increasing for the musical results Alex was achieving with few words and slight gestures. She made a mental note to practice the tricky places before the next rehearsal. She certainly didn't look forward to evoking audible groans like those she heard from the oboist during the violins' most ragged struggles. She winced at his *sotto voce* comments when the first bassoon dragged behind and hit repeated sour notes in the woodwind choir's answer to the horns.

"Lumbering elephant," he muttered, just too loudly to be misunderstood.

At last the violas—and everyone else—were invited back into the fray, and the first movement concluded in relative triumph.

"Not bad, for the first rehearsal," Alex pronounced. "We'll read the last movement next week, I think, and work on the second. We might even get to the overture."

The discipline of rehearsal dissolved into general chatter and packing up. Yoichi meandered from stand to stand picking up registration cards and the music folders of the confident few who weren't signing them out.

"Do we need to do anything about stands and seats?" Joan asked her partner.

"Audition? Sure, if you want to. I'm not going to bother. Alex knows how I sound, and I have no ambition to sit first."

"No, I'm happy. I meant the chairs themselves."

"Just leave 'em. I don't know how long it's been since anyone here has had to help set up. Some people are even beginning to agitate for pay."

"Maybe I'm out of my league."

"You're fine. I was listening. Say, could you take the music this week and let me have it next time? I know I won't get a chance between now and next Wednesday."

"Thanks. I was hoping I could."

The stage was clearing rapidly, but at the narrow steps Joan recognized the string bass player whose descent was causing a minor traffic jam.

"Come on, shorty, move it," said a curly-headed man holding a small case and patting his foot. It was the super-critical first oboe player. Below him, the little man stopped dead, set down the bass, and looked up.

"Just go, will you?" snapped the oboist. "Maybe you ought to take up the piccolo. Then we'd all get home on time."

Jaw clenched, the pudgy bassist shoved his stool aside at the bottom of the stairs to clear the path. Joan stood speechless as the oboe player hurried down the steps and out the door.

At her shoulder, Alex Campbell said quietly, "If I auditioned on any basis but music, he'd be out. In fact, if *he* played piccolo, I wouldn't put up with him. But a good oboe isn't easy to come by."

"It's really true, isn't it? An oboe is an ill wind that nobody blows good."

Alex groaned. "I haven't heard that one in years. And I haven't met you."

"Don't hold it against me, please. I'm Joan Spencer. I play viola."

"Don't worry. We're almost as short of violas this year as we are of oboes. I hope you won't let this keep you away. He's a fine musician, but tact is not his long suit."

"It won't matter. He's not conducting. I did enjoy this evening. It's been a while since I've had a place to play."

Below them, the bassist had recovered his equilibrium. Joan remembered that she owed him something and went down to thank him for guiding her in. "If it hadn't been for you, I don't think I'd have made the first half."

"I wondered if you were new," he said.

"New? She lived here before you knew where Oliver was on the map." It was Nancy. "Harold Williams, this is Joan Zimmerman. We're old friends."

"It's Joan Spencer now, Nancy."

"Of course. And I'm not a Krebs anymore. I'll tell you all about it."

# Chapter Two

By the time they settled down in Nancy's roomy kitchen, they had covered most of the vital statistics. Nancy's husband, a quiet professor, retreated into his study as soon as he could without open insult. Joan wondered whether her son Andrew would ever take a course from him at Oliver College, but she knew better than to mention the possibility.

Cats dominated the childless household. A flat-faced, gray longhair blanketed the top of the refrigerator and a tabby kitten wound back and forth between them, rubbing against their legs. A calico that had materialized from somewhere now lay on the newspaper abandoned by the professor. Nancy complained about them in the tones of a doting mother. "Emily over there is death on newspapers. Makes it hard to check my work."

"You write for the paper?"

"No, don't you remember? I draw—always did. I have a nice little business doing local advertising art. Everything from nightgowns to canoes. Not the kind of thing you'd hang on your wall, but it pays well, and I'm good, if I do say so."

"I'm job hunting, myself. No talent, I'm afraid. Just dull capability. I keep hoping someone will recognize it."

Joan could see the wheels begin to turn. Well, fine, although she hadn't meant to hint.

"Don't worry about it, Nancy. Tell me about people. It feels so strange to be back in a place I was sure I'd never forget and not to see a soul I know. Even the elm trees have disappeared, and the old school. What's the same?"

"Everything. It's the same old town, only older. Miss Duffy still lives on Beech Street. She'd be tickled pink to see you."

"And people our age?"

"They're mostly long gone. Gilbert Snarr is still here, running his dad's funeral home, and Bob Peterson works at the paper."

"I'll bet you're the only person I'll know, except for Miss Duffy. I'll have to find her."

"Oh, and Evelyn. Did you see her checking you out at the symphony break?"

"Evelyn?"

"You remember Evelyn Gustafson." It wasn't a question. Joan began to remember that it almost never was with Nancy, not a real one.

"No, I don't think so."

"Oh, you can't have forgotten her. Anything she did was always better and more important than our affairs. She wore ballet slippers and crinolines to school, and she could fast dance when the rest of us were trying to figure out the box step. Made me green. Evelyn married Sam Wade from Fish Creek—well, maybe you didn't know Sam.

"Anyway, Evelyn and Sam had a thing going even in junior high. She was unbearable when he gave her his high school class ring. Don't you remember? One day she'd wrap it with blue angora yarn, and the next day it was all tape and nail polish. Anything for an excuse to wave it at the rest of us."

"Mmm." Joan smothered a yawn.

"I knew it would come back to you. She was so smug, even then. When he was training for a chance at the Olympics, she was just like all the girls in the Charles Atlas ad, hanging around the guy with the beautiful muscles, only she had the inside track. And you should have heard her when he went away to school where he could swim outdoors all year long under some famous coach. I think maybe it's the high school Mark Spitz went to. Of course, *he* came here to Indiana for college before he won all those golds. Isn't he a dentist or something? I hear he's never swum again since. Anyway, Sam didn't last long. He dropped it, just like that, I never heard why, and went into the army or the marines, I forget which, and then to IU on the GI Bill. When he came back with a law degree, Evelyn wasn't worth speaking to—much too good for the rest of us.

"After a while, though, wills and contracts and such weren't exciting enough. It got them into the country club, though, and that's Evelyn's meat. And now that he's in politics, she's busy helping him by helping us."

"You lost me back at the wills and contracts."

"Sorry. Sam got himself elected county prosecutor and now he has his eye on a seat in Congress. Then on to bigger and better things, at least if you listen to Evelyn. She doesn't say all that, of course. But she manages to make him sound important at the same time she's putting down not only the job he has now, but the one he's going to run for next."

"What did you mean about helping us?"

"She's got herself in solid with the symphony. It doesn't matter who really licked the stamps. It always ends up looking as if Evelyn did it single-handed. You watch—at break time, she's right in there handing out all the cookies someone else baked. Didn't you recognize her tonight?"

"Not really," Joan said, stifling another yawn. "People have changed a lot since the sixth grade. I don't think I really remember them at all."

"Well, of course not. Silly of me. Sam was Giddy then."

"She sounds like the giddy one."

"No, his name was Giddy—short for Gideon. I think he started using his middle name when he decided to be a lawyer. It always embarrassed Evelyn. But I suppose she was right. Who'd want a giddy lawyer? These days I notice she has him using all three— like William Howard Taft or Norman Vincent Peale. You remember how she was."

"No, Nancy, I don't," Joan said firmly. "Most all of that must have happened after I left. I seem to have blocked Evelyn out of my life."

"Well, you can't miss her. Here we all are at our grubbiest and there she is with every hair in place. She'll fall all over you if she thinks you can do Sam some good."

"Who, me? I'll probably never even meet the man."

"Oh, I don't know about that. You're sitting next to him."

"I don't think so," Joan answered, puzzled. "The man I'm next to introduced himself and that wasn't his name. It was something to do with beer glasses."

"Beer glasses?"

"I should never have said that out loud. I'm learning so many new names right now—addresses, phone numbers—and my old memory system isn't working. He's bald, has a nice smile."

"John Hocking!"

"So much for that system."

"I didn't mean John. Sam's the oboe on your right."

"That awful man who chewed out the bassist for living? Harold somebody?"

"No, Harold's the bass. Runs Aqua Heaven. We bought our saltwater tank from him. Sam plays second oboe. The boor is George Petris. He sits first, and he's just bad news. Although some women manage to find him charming, how I don't know. His wife stuck it out almost twenty years before she couldn't take any more of his playing around, and I don't mean oboe. And last year he stole his own son's best girl. For a while it looked as if Lisa might actually end up as stepmother to her old boyfriend. But George dumped her and she took off sometime last winter—just left town. She's back now, but she not only won't speak to George— she won't give the time of day to any man. You can imagine what people are saying. The sad part is that I think those kids really cared about each other. And Daniel is all right. His mother's influence, I suppose."

"You don't like the man."

"You guessed it. Anyway, Sam's not like George at all, thank goodness. One of him is enough. Besides, Sam's much too good a politician to be rude unintentionally."

"I'll look next week. Tonight went by in a blur." Blurrier by the minute. She felt herself droop with sudden fatigue. Even Nancy noticed.

"Joan, you're tired and I'm just running on. I do remember how it feels. The last sabbatical Art took was the longest year I've ever spent. Never seeing people I knew, not even at the grocery store, just wore me out. I'd never survive in a big city. But I'll bet that after a while some of the faces on the street here will begin to ring a bell for you. And I'll be happy to tell you about people. It really helps if you know their backgrounds, don't you think?"

Joan ducked it. "Nancy, you're right, I am tired. I'll see you next week."

The chatter followed her out to the car. She started the motor and waved, pretending not to have heard the beginning of still another long story.

Soon, however, she would be wishing she could remember exactly what Nancy had told her about George Petris and his affairs.

# Chapter Three

Joan struggled to match the oboe's ever more insistent A, but she couldn't budge the peg. Pushing with all her strength, she felt it suddenly give. The string snapped in her face, the bridge flew into a dark corner, the sound post collapsed, and the oboe rose to an unbearable wail. With her hand resisting her efforts to loosen the other strings and relieve the tension on the viola's now unsupported belly, she screamed aloud, "Stop it! I can't!"

Sudden silence. Blessed relief.

Then a voice in her ear.

"Mom, are you okay?"

Lethargy.

"Mom, wake up."

She opened her eyes. "Andrew. I was having a nightmare."

"Really. You were yelping."

Already the panic had faded. She worked to remember. "I couldn't tune my viola."

"That's a nightmare?"

"Silly, isn't it? But that oboe kept screaming at me." Probably the nasty one. George What-sis.

"Uh, Mom, I think I'm your oboe. I put the toast in the broken side of the toaster, and the smoke alarm blew while I was scrambling eggs. It took me a minute to climb up there and shut it off. I didn't think anyone could sleep through that, not even you."

"I wasn't exactly sleeping."

"Sorry. But you were really out of it. How late did you come home last night?"

"Hey, who's the parent around here?"

Andrew beetled his brows and reached down for his deepest baritone. "How late?"

"Very late. I met an old friend, and we talked our heads off. Or rather, she talked and I listened."

"Some excuse."

"No excuse. But I learned a couple of things."

"Like?"

"Oh, mostly that almost no one I used to know is still here. Except my teacher."

"From sixth grade?"

"Back in the Dark Ages. Miss Duffy's probably one of the reasons I think of Oliver as home. She was a born teacher, Andrew."

"I could use one of those."

"Oh, that's another thing I learned. My friend is Nancy Van Allen. Her husband teaches chemistry at the college."

"What's he like?"

"Smart enough to go to bed on time. He didn't sit in on all our talk. Nice enough, as far as I could tell."

"Well, Haynes won't be, if I'm late for school again. You want some cold eggs?"

"Andrew, I'm sorry."

"It's okay. I can get something later. I'll see you at suppertime. Bye, Mom."

Grateful for the how-manyeth time that this echo of his father was very much his own person, she got up to watch him bicycle off, curly head bent and long legs pumping.

She was certainly wide awake now. Cold eggs held no appeal, but the morning paper might get her moving. She scuffled into the slippers that had been a stopgap a year ago, wrapped her robe around her warmly on the way downstairs, put the teakettle on, and retrieved the *Courier* from behind the bushes. Again.

Brushing the dew-laden cobweb from her eyebrow, she plunged into the "help wanted" section. Waded in was closer to it. The bottom was so near the surface that a real dive would have flattened her. "Loving person to care for four active children in my home." "Experienced legal secretary 80 wpm." "L.P.N. for busy physician's office." "Couple to live in residential treatment center for troubled youth."

One advantage to being unemployed—you didn't have to rush breakfast. With a feeling of total self-indulgence, she scraped Andrew's eggs into the garbage and then took her time over a muffin and the funnies. After a quick call to the employment agency yielded no more leads, she set herself free for the day.

The phone book listed three Duffys—only one on Beech Street. What did M. E. stand for? She must have known once, but it wouldn't come.

"Miss Duffy? This is Joan Zimmerman. I was a pupil of yours years ago. I don't know if you'll remember...How very nice of you to say so. No, I'm not visiting. I'll be living here for a few years, I think. Could I come by to see you? Why, yes, I could easily be there at ten, if I don't get lost."

She didn't. Already she had learned that in a town the size of Oliver, she could save her gasoline money. Walking gave her time to get her bearings. And there was something even simpler. The last time she had lived there, driving hadn't been one of her options. No wonder everything looked more familiar from the sidewalk.

Halfway down a long block she recognized Miss Duffy standing on the front porch of the little house she had occupied for so many years. Feet solidly planted, she conveyed by her very posture the calm that had always given her control over rambunctious children. She had never shouted, never sent anyone to the office, never called the principal. Her snapping eyes and that steady calm had done it, plus a quick, quiet wit that stopped just short of scolding.

Miss Duffy must have spotted her, but she just waited on the porch. It fits, Joan thought. On the other hand, how would she know me? I've changed far more than she has.

"Hello," she called, turning onto the little brick path to the house. "It's me, Joan."

"Come here, Joan. Let me look at you. I'm so glad you called."

Joan returned her hug warmly.

She had visited the house on children's errands: selling Girl Scout cookies, trick-or-treating, looking for a yard to rake or a walk to shovel to augment an allowance too skimpy for a movie ticket and popcorn. Today she was welcomed as an adult. And with Margaret Duffy—the "Margaret" came easily as soon as she was invited to use it—she felt like one. The feeling that this was a person who cared about her hadn't changed it all. Yet Margaret Duffy's kind of caring didn't hover; it sat back and waited.

Somewhat to her own surprise, Joan found herself explaining about Ken's death, Andrew's interest in Oliver College, her decision to move to the little house her parents had bought years ago for the retirement they'd never been able to enjoy, and her search for a job.

"What have you done?" Margaret asked, hands folded over her ample lap, little feet crossed in the trim shoes.

"A motley assortment of things. Research assistant jobs before the children were born. A lot of volunteer work after that. Playing in the orchestra for fun, when we lived where there was one. I'm doing that here, too. And then when I had to support us, I learned about the difference between jobs that sound good and the ones that pay. You find out who your friends are when you show up in the A&P as a checker. Some of Ken's former parishioners thought it was beneath the dignity of their minister's widow. They didn't offer to pay the bills, you understand—just fussed at me about finding something 'more suitable.' I don't think they'd have been bothered if I'd taken a part-time job in the library and starved."

"Did you put them to the test?" The eyes had their old familiar gleam.

"It crossed my mind a time or two. For one thing, my feet hurt. But finally, one of Ken's ministerial colleagues offered me a job in his church. The congregation is big enough to pay almost a living wage to the church secretary—administrative assistant, really—and they wanted someone who wouldn't carry gossip back to the members. Gossip bores me silly; he may have known that. And I suppose he thought I'd know enough about the inner workings of that situation to do a good job. He was right. It didn't occur to me that he might have any other motive, and I'm not even sure he did. I thought it would be fine. For a while, it was."

"But you're here."

"I never expected to leave. I really did like the work. It wasn't very hard, but it took an organized mind and all the diplomacy I could command to keep the nursery school out of the hair of the Tuesday morning circle meeting, and the choir director from coming to blows with the Boy Scouts."

"Mm-hmm." Still, Margaret Duffy didn't push it.

"But I'm here," Joan said wryly. "And with no job at all. It doesn't make sense, does it?"

"Do you want me to ask you why?"

"No. Yes. I don't know." And then it came rushing out, all that she had kept bottled up for months. How the minister, an old friend whose marriage had always seemed solid, had pursued her. How his attentions, at first no more than flattering, had become intolerable, until the day she had fended him off with the letter opener from the engraved desk set presented to him by the last confirmation class.

"I went home in the middle of the day, shaking. I was scared and angry—I don't think I've ever been so angry in my life."

"What did you do about it?" There was the old Miss Duffy calm.

"At first I was too upset to do anything. I paced. I must have gone up and down the stairs a dozen times in half an hour. I told myself I was making a mountain out of a molehill. I didn't tell anyone about it, not even Andrew. Least of all Andrew. Finally I thought I had it all under control. Then, the next morning, when I tried to go to work, I found I couldn't leave the house. I simply couldn't turn the doorknob. And I realized that no matter what he did the next time, I wasn't sure what I would do if I went near him—and that letter opener. So I resigned, and we moved."

"You left town without telling anyone?" Margaret spoke gently, but Joan found it difficult to respond.

"I ran. I'm not proud of that. But Margaret, that man is almost a saint in the eyes of his congregation. He's had community awards galore. No one would believe my word against his. Oh, I was angry enough to want to punish him, but it wouldn't have worked that way. The whole town would have been convinced that I was a sex-starved widow, making it up because I really wanted it to be true. And there was no way I could stay in town and not be thrown together with him—and his wife."

"You may be right."

"Right or wrong, I'm looking for a job here. I have to hang onto what's left of Ken's insurance money for Andrew's college tuition. I was counting on Social Security for some of that, but the new rules will cut him off on his eighteenth birthday."

"There aren't many jobs here," Margaret said. "Students do a lot of them. Do you have trouble because of your age?"

"My age?" A new worry she didn't even want to consider.

"It's the kind of thing you hear a lot at the Senior Citizens' Center. You know, Joan..." She paused. "Why don't you apply for the job at the center?"

"Is one open?"

"The board's been looking a week now. The director resigned suddenly, and she's given us no notice at all. We need an acting director within the week. No one who is assisting is willing or appropriate for the job, and I think you'd bring something to it that those children can't."

"Now you're discriminating on account of age."

"Not entirely, but I can't think of a better place to do it."

"I don't quite know what to say."

"How do you feel about spending time with old people?"

"Just old, or old and sick?"

"Just old. Well, we all have more creaks and leaks than we once did, but the people who come to the center are in fairly good health, at least when they come. Some of us are as sharp as we ever were and some aren't." She smiled. "Some weren't all that sharp to begin with, of course."

Going over to a neat desk, she brought Joan a mimeographed folder. "Here's a list of our programs. And I wonder...You might know one of our regulars, from the orchestra. Have you met Elmer Rush?"

"The bassoon player? He said he'd moved here to be near his daughter and grandchildren."

"That's the one. He spends all day with his granddaughter while her mother works. She's in her twenties—the granddaughter, I mean—but she's retarded. There was a water accident when she was very young, and they managed to revive her just too late, or just too soon, some people say. Sometimes he brings her to the center. It gives him a chance to talk to adults during the day. That's why a lot of people come. A husband or wife is senile or ill, or dead, and they feel lost."

"Mm-hmm. It's lonely." She remembered how empty the house had felt without Ken, in spite of two active children.

"Yes," said Margaret, "even for people like me, who are used to living alone. Your friends keep dying. Young people arrange all the right things, but they haven't lived long enough to know what we're missing. Some of them talk to all of us as if we had lost our minds."

"Before my husband died, I thought I knew what being widowed must be like, but you know, I had no idea at all. I'm sure I don't know what it's like to be older than everyone around me, either."

"But you know you don't know. Just think it over. I'll be glad to dredge up an old report card, if you need a reference." Her mouth twitched at the corners.

Down, girl, Joan told herself. You don't even know their requirements, much less what they pay. But her relief at a real possibility outweighed any such sensible concerns. She collected herself enough to answer.

"Margaret, thank you for telling me about it. Even if it's only temporary, it could mean a lot to me and to Andrew."

"If you're serious, I'll bring up your name tonight. Then you can apply tomorrow."

"Oh, would you please?" The child in Joan had already begun to celebrate. Maybe you can go home again after all, she thought.

# Chapter Four

Nancy climbed into the car with her mouth open. "It's been quite a week. How are you? I'm just worn out. This is the only week the painter could come, and you know how that turns everything upside down. He brings assistants and they spread out all through the house. No matter where I go to try to get something done, they've covered everything in sight. I'm putting new curtains in our room—the color is completely different. And you just can't find decent lining in Oliver, or three-inch buckram for the heading. I went all the way to Bloomington for that. They're turning out rather well, though, if I do say so. I finally told the painters they could have my sewing room or my workroom, but not both at once. That's the only way I've managed at all. Every time they give a coat of paint another day to dry, I have to switch from curtains to a big Halloween layout I'm doing."

She paused just long enough to register Joan's surprise. "September isn't early at all for Halloween. I'm already working on Christmas. Oh, and Joan, are you still looking for a job? Because I've been talking with the manager and I think I've found you at least a little one, if you'll have it."

Joan smiled, ready to share her news. "Well," she said, but Nancy cut in quickly.

"Don't say no until you've heard. It isn't much money, but it isn't much work, either, just a few hours every week, and some of them you'd be using anyway."

"Nancy, what are you talking about?"

"The librarian's job. For the orchestra. We finally have the funds to pay someone to do properly what we've been messing up b'guess and b'gosh for years. You order the music, with Alex, of course, and take charge of it when it comes. We have some of our own, but whatever we rent or borrow has to be returned on time and erased, or we're socked with fines. Someone's always losing a part. If it turns up a month later, it might as well not turn up at all. You'd need a better system than we have now. And you'd do odds and ends for Yoichi Nakamura—he's the manager. A Japanese student. He said a couple of words last week, remember? The pay's low, but after all, you're not doing anything else, and it might help some."

"It might at that. But you're wrong about one thing."

"Oh?"

"I am doing something else. Since Monday. I'm acting director at the Senior Citizens' Center." She enjoyed the look on Nancy's face.

"Well, for heaven's sake! You certainly didn't waste any time. How did you find out about it?"

"As a matter of fact, you sent me to it, when you told me Margaret Duffy was still in town. She's my insider. Nancy, it's only been three days and I have a lot to learn, but I think I'm going to like it. If I really fit in, there's a chance that I'll get to stay. On the other hand, I don't see why I couldn't do the orchestra job in the evenings. How do I apply?"

"Oh, that's easy. The orchestra has been asking around and getting no takers for about a month. Tell Alex you're willing and I'm sure it's yours."

At this rate, Joan thought, I could expect the bank presidency to fall into my lap by next month. Nancy was already back to debating wallpaper in the stairwell.

In the parking lot they pulled up beside an old green Volkswagen Rabbit. Joan recognized Elmer's shock of white hair. So he had made it past the tryouts.

"You survived."

"I did. Not only that, I'm sitting first. How's that for an old man?"

"That's great, but seventy isn't so old." She grinned at him.

"I don't remember bragging on my age to you."

"No, I peeked. Congratulations, Elmer. The new acting director of the Senior Citizens' Center is proud of you."

"Well, then, we'll have a chance to get to know each other. Congratulations to us both." He shook her hand warmly.

Onstage, congratulations were restrained at best. Earrings clinking, the former first bassoonist managed a civility that fell a few hundred yards short of cordiality. Joan hoped that Elmer could weather the miffed feelings and that his musicianship would justify a decision to bump someone with seniority in the orchestra. Amateur egos, she knew, were no less touchy then those of the pros. Maybe more so. At least professionals could soothe their wounded self-esteem with cash. Amateurs were all too likely to be donating to the very group that demoted them.

Other seating seemed to raise no eyebrows. From her vague memories of the week before, Joan thought most of the prominent players were the ones she had seen then. Nancy would know, of course, or John Hocking. She found Alex and was welcomed warmly as librarian and manager's assistant, as Nancy had predicted. The job paid a thousand dollars a season—no pittance after all. Diving right in, she helped distribute folders and barely had time to tune before the rehearsal began in earnest.

They read the breakneck last movement of the Schubert, she hoped almost up to tempo. To her chagrin, Joan found that the little practice she had managed in her hectic week of interviews and first, unexpected days at work had been spent on the wrong places. She penciled scribbly stars beside the most glaring difficulties, wondering if she'd ever be able to do them justice.

Then, back they went to the violins' problems. Books and knitting reappeared. Empty-handed again, Joan remembered that she had meant to check out the player married to her old classmate. The oboes had their reed knives and sandpaper out again. Bent to his task, Sam Wade didn't meet her eyes. No wonder the man chose a political career, she thought. That handsome face and wavy hair, graying over the temples, had to be worth at least ten percent of the vote. He'd be the bane of the political cartoonists, though. No feature was irregular enough to caricature. They'd have to label his briefcase or stick a little flag in his hand.

Beyond him she saw George Petris beginning to wind the base of his double reed. And wonder of wonders, Elmer had won him over. At least, they had their heads together and George seemed to be demonstrating his technique. Suddenly, almost fiercely, Alex tapped for quiet. George finished a sentence in full voice, but Elmer quickly leaned forward and slipped the bassoon reed he was making into a bottle to soak. He sat very still, his face reddening. Not wanting to embarrass him, Joan looked away.

Playing or waiting, she was very warm. She mopped her eyebrows with the handkerchief that kept her chin and chin rest from floating apart on a puddle of perspiration.

At intermission, even the awful punch appealed. Yoichi approached her, asking apologetically if she would pass out some new parts during the break. Crunching on an ice cube, by far the best part of the punch, she worked her way around the sections.

It was easier than passing out folders before the rehearsal, because almost everyone had left for a drink or a breath of outside air. The horn chorale haunted her again and the trumpeter was attacking a concerto. John Hocking's daughter, pointed out by her father, was working on her geometry, pencil clenched and tongue between her teeth. Joan slipped the music into her folder, but the girl didn't look up.

When Joan came past the flutes to the oboe section, where Sam Wade was drying his pads with cigarette papers slipped under the keys, her foot tangled with a chair leg and she landed almost in his lap, sending the chair and a stand crashing, music flying, and a reed bottle spinning.

"Are you hurt?" He helped her up.

"Only my dignity." She wished it were true. She hadn't changed clothes since work; one pair of stockings had just joined her stockpile for staking up tomatoes. Almost worth adding to the tomato stakers—watch it, Joan, she thought. He's married, and to a very possessive lady, if I heard Nancy right.

"What klutz dumped my music?" roared a familiar voice behind her.

"Oh, go klutz yourself," she heard herself answering. "It's all there."

Quickly, she set the stand on its foot, collected the pages, added the new ones, and stood the bottle up. She hoped its lid had protected the fragile reeds. She knew how temperamental they could be, and she could imagine what George Petris would say if one of those reeds failed him later. Without looking back at either man, she moved on with the music.

John Hocking was chuckling when she returned to her seat. "I've never seen him at a loss for words before," he told her. "He's not used to people who don't lie down and play dead."

"I'd like to see him muzzled. No one has a right to be so ugly to people." Her own indignation annoyed her. Music, she reminded herself. That's why I came.

Her annoyance increased when she realized that there would be no tuning for the second half. The break had run too long, and the concertmaster was among the laggards Yoichi was shooing in from the cool evening air. Alex didn't wait, but began with the violins and violas.

"Let's take it from the top of the second movement. There are a lot of you, but I want to hear you sound like one instrument. Be with my beat immediately and keep it steady—no accents—just like a machine. It's only piano, but I'll need a little more from the cellos and basses after the third bar." She turned to them. "That's where you have something to say."

With all the hard things in this symphony, thought Joan, here we are rehearsing pom-poms. But by the fourth time through the first few measures, she could hear why. What a simple thing, she thought, and what a difference!

"Now with everybody, please."

Pom-pom-pom-pom, pom-pom-pom-pom, steady as a rock. The cellos and basses introduced the little theme. Then, with the first oboe note, the pom-poms obediently dropped to a well-defined whisper. But the oboe was all wrong, off pitch, lagging behind the beat. Serves him right, Joan thought smugly. Abruptly, he broke off altogether.

Alex's face changed from business to concern. "George, are you all right?"

He tried to answer, but he couldn't seem to work his mouth. "Num," Joan heard him say, into silence as sudden as a General Pause. He was sitting in an odd position, holding his oboe awkwardly. As he spoke, it began to slip from his fingers. The flutist to his right caught it before it could hit the floor.

"He's sick!" she exclaimed. Sam leaned over to support him from the left.

"He needs an ambulance, fast. How far are we from the hospital?" asked Elmer, behind him.

"Not far, but the phones here are all locked up," answered John. "I'll take him."

"I'll help you," Yoichi offered.

"George, I'll take care of your oboe for you. Don't worry about a thing," the flutist told him. He managed to nod in her direction. John and Yoichi half-supported, half-carried him from the stage.

The general hubbub of concern among the remaining members of the orchestra lacked a certain warmth. No one said, "Poor George, I hope he's all right." Comments tended more toward: "He was fine during the break; I talked to him" and "Where'll we get another oboe if he's not back by the concert?" and "Looks like a stroke, or some kind of seizure, whaddya think?" Alex cut through the chatter to ask who knew George's son.

"Glenda ought to," someone answered and was promptly shushed.

"I know Daniel," volunteered the flutist who had saved the oboe.

"Good. Would you phone him, Wanda? As for the rest of us, I doubt that we'll do much in the next half hour. Let's call it a night."

Joan sat staring at George's empty seat, watching Wanda pack up for him and feeling what she knew was a childish guilt at seeing her wish come true. The boor had certainly been muzzled. Much as she disliked the man, she couldn't wish sudden collapse on anyone. No use dwelling on it; she might as well take care of John's viola, which he'd left on his chair, and see what else she should do to close up, since Yoichi was gone too.

"Are you all right?" Sam Wade swiveled to look at her. "You took quite a fall a while back."

"Yes, I'm fine. Just a little startled." In the back of her mind she realized why. The scene she had just witnessed reminded her all too vividly of her young husband's sudden heart attack. Mustn't think of that right now.

"You're Sam Wade, aren't you?" she made herself ask. "I'm told I went to school with your wife."

"College?"

"No, elementary school. Nancy Van Allen says we were all three in the same class."

"Let's see if Evelyn remembers." He looked around vaguely and then spotted the woman whose elegance had struck Joan the week before. A slight jerk of his head brought her to them, at her own high-heeled pace.

"Evelyn, this is—but I forgot to ask your name." His rueful smile melted her.

"Joan Zimmerman—at least that's who I was back in Miss Duffy's sixth grade, I hate to think how many years ago. Nancy tells me you were there, too."

"How interesting. What brings you to Oliver?" The queen greeting the commoner.

"We needed a change and my son wanted to look over the college for next year." Pretty lame, but Evelyn didn't seem to notice.

"Poor boy, he'll have to live in a dormitory. He can't move into a fraternity until his sophomore year, you know."

"I don't think he'll do that." I'm not about to tell this one he might have to live at home, or why, Joan thought.

"Sam's a Mu Tau Kappa man. It's the best on campus. Your son really should get to know those young men."

"I'll mention it to Andrew."

Evelyn turned her back ever so subtly.

"Sam, dear, what happened to George Petris? I was helping Glenda put the refreshment supplies in her car when they brought him out and drove off. He looked terrible."

"I don't know. He was fine one minute and then he couldn't play at all."

"He never could play as well as you. I still don't understand why you're willing to sit second to him. You know, Joan, Sam is a superb musician. The orchestra is lucky to have him. It's sad that he'll probably have even less time for it next year than he does now."

Joan didn't let her have the satisfaction of explaining.

"I'm sorry to hear that. Music is a joy to me. I'd hate to crowd it out of my life. But speaking of time, I should let you go. I still have a job to do here. Thank you, Sam, for picking me up. See you next week."

She left them and began collecting folders, irritated at herself for letting the woman bother her, but not altogether dissatisfied with what she'd done about it. She noticed that almost everyone had left. Alex came to ask if she needed help.

"Thanks, I think I'll be fine. What do you suggest I do about John's viola?"

"Yoichi left his violin, too. I imagine they'll both come back here. If you're finished before they come, would you be willing to take the instruments and leave them a note? The janitor stays until ten. They'll be able to get in until then. You might check with them in the morning if they haven't called you."

"Sure. I'll see you next week, then."

Alex trundled off. Joan wished she'd remembered to ask whether the janitor was paid to clean up after some of the messier players. She found Styrofoam cups, some still containing dregs of punch and an occasional cigarette butt, under a number of seats. Nancy, coming for her ride home, helped her toss the mess into the trash. They decided that the shavings around the oboes' seats were certainly the janitor's job, but Joan picked up the little bottle of reeds she had kicked earlier. She found the lid on the floor and screwed it on tightly so that it wouldn't leak onto the music in the librarian's box.

Just as they were leaving, John arrived. He couldn't tell them much. "Yoichi sat in the back seat with him. I drove."

"It was good of you to go."

"I hope so. I'm afraid he might have been better off if we'd found a way to call an ambulance after all. By the time we got there, he was having a terrible time breathing. Yoichi said his uncle died just like that. He took George right into the emergency room. I only hope they didn't make him wait."

"Why should he have to wait?"

"He shouldn't, of course. It's not like Saturday night. Although, if enough doctors take Wednesday afternoon off, the place is sometimes pretty busy on Wednesday night. I broke a foot once on a Wednesday and I recommend choosing another day."

"They're fairly conservative around here," said Nancy. "There's someone on duty, but they'd much rather wait to treat you until your own physician meets you at the hospital."

"I certainly hope he's all right. Are we ready to go?"

Nancy's self-absorbed chatter let Joan retreat into her own thoughts on the way home. In the house, she dumped the music box in a corner, slid her viola and Yoichi's violin under a table, and flopped into a big chair.

For the first time in months, she unloaded on Andrew.

"It was so...cold. They did all the right things, but nobody seemed to care. Nobody acted as if he mattered. Just their precious music and their own social climbing. I don't know if I want to go back to that bunch, Andrew."

"Are they all that bad?"

"I don't know. I suppose not. It just made me feel sick inside."

"You're thinking about Dad, aren't you?" He hugged her. "He'd tell them where to get off."

She smiled. Andrew still idolized his father as a dragon slayer, at war with pomposity and afraid of no one.

It was true, Joan thought. Year after year, in one parish after another, Ken had stood up to trustees and committees with the moral courage that had sent him marching to Selma in 1965, young and armed only with his unshakable belief in a just cause. She had never tried to stop him, whether it was his job or his life that he put in danger. His death, when it came, had given her no warning after all.

Joan ducked quarrels. The family joke had been "Dad insists on his way, but Mom gets hers." But that had been easy, with Ken to run interference for her. Now tears threatened. She blew her nose loudly.

"I thought I was past all that a long time ago. I'm sorry, Andrew. I didn't mean to do that to you."

"Any time, Mom."

"You're probably right. John and Yoichi were just great. After all, most people who get sick do recover. I'm probably the only one who doesn't expect George to be back and twice as nasty next week."

# Chapter Five

Yoichi showed up on her doorstep while she was eating breakfast. Joan opened the door wide.

"Come in and have a cup of coffee. I don't have to leave for half an hour."

"Thank you. If it isn't any trouble, I would like that." He didn't smile or look at her.

"No trouble at all. Here you are." She set a steaming mug before him and pushed the sweet rolls in his direction. "Help yourself to a napkin. I gather you got my note."

He sat very still for a moment. "Note? No, I didn't receive any note."

"I left one at the school. All it said was that I had your violin." She pulled it out from under the table. He took it and ducked his head at her.

"I hoped you would know where it was. I came to ask and to thank you. I left you with all the work." That stillness again. He slid the double zipper tabs on the canvas case cover back and forth absently.

"I was glad to do something. How is George, Yoichi?"

His face answered her before his voice could. "George died in the emergency room last night."

"Oh, Yoichi, I am so very sorry." Memories threatened her composure again. Hang on, she thought. Don't go all soggy.

"So am I. They tried to make him breathe again, but they couldn't."

"Was his son there?" Someone—Wanda, the flutist—had gone to call him.

"Daniel came too late."

"What happened, do they know?"

"No, they don't know. And I don't understand how it could happen here."

"What do you mean, here?"

"My Uncle Katsuo died in the same way, in Japan. There they recognized immediately what caused his death. It was *fugu sashimi.*"

"Foogoo...?"

"It is a very special fish. It is served raw, prepared in beautiful designs. But part of the fish is a powerful poison. Only people who know exactly how to clean the fish are licensed to prepare the *sashimi.*"

Oh, *fugu.* She'd read about it somewhere.

"I remember now. There's a photograph in one of my cookbooks. And something about a tingle. Don't some people think the tingle comes from the excitement of eating something that could be dangerous?"

"It is real, if any of the poison remains in the fish. But after the tingle, the mouth becomes numb, without feeling, and then the limbs also lose their feeling and control. Finally breathing stops, the heart stops, and the person dies."

"Numb—that's what George said."

"Excuse me, please?" He leaned forward intently.

"When George stopped playing, he said 'num.' I thought it was only part of a word."

"Then I am certain. I told the doctors and one of them took me seriously, I think. He is *nisei*—Japanese-American. But by the time he saw George, many poisons could have caused his symptoms."

"Can't they test for it?"

His forehead wrinkled. "I asked them to. But I am afraid it will not be possible."

"Surely, if he ate the fish, they could find the fish."

"That is why I think they do not believe me. Daniel Petris told them his father hates—hated fish. They ate dinner at a steak house before the rehearsal, he says."

"Is Daniel truthful?" she asked.

"As you say, the doctors will soon know what he ate. But I have seen only two people ill in this way. I don't understand it."

"Yoichi, were you with your uncle when he died?"

"Yes. We had spent the day together fishing. We often caught small *fugu*, but he usually threw them back. That day we caught a big one he thought he could prepare safely. It is a great delicacy—very expensive in a restaurant. He refused to let me take the risk, because I was only fifteen. He was my favorite uncle."

"I know how you must be feeling." She told him how George's sudden collapse had evoked feelings about her husband's fatal attack.

For the first time, Yoichi showed signs of anger. His voice rose in pitch, and his careful pronunciation of L and R failed him.

"You think I remember my uncle's death so strongly that I was imagining this similarity?"

"Not imagining. But don't you think there are other illnesses that would cause such symptoms?" I'm not helping him at all, she thought. Why should I try to argue with him? "We may never know just how George died," she tried.

"That is not what concerns me."

"Then…"

"If I am right and Daniel is telling the truth, then George did not just die. He was murdered."

Oh, my, she thought. He's more upset than I realized. "Did you suggest that possibility to the doctors?"

"Yes, I did."

"What did they say?"

"Very little. I don't think they will do anything. I think they believe it is my imagination."

"Yoichi, if you truly believe that somebody may have murdered George Petris you must go to the police. Or…"

"Yes?"

"I wonder. Isn't Sam Wade the prosecutor? Couldn't you ask him to investigate? I don't know if that's the way things are usually done, but since he's in the orchestra—he sat right next to George, for goodness sake—he would surely want to help."

Yoichi stared at her, too startled for Japanese courtesy.

"Of course. I should have thought of him." He remembered his manners, glanced away, and thanked her for the untouched coffee and for keeping his violin. "Please excuse me."

She saw him to the door, wondering how much of all this could have anything to do with reality. Surely no one would send to Japan for poisonous fish to commit a murder, much less hide it in a steak. It all sounded very strange, but Yoichi seemed much more in control of himself, and she was glad to have offered him a way to do something.

George Petris murdered. She'd felt tempted herself a time or two. But, as she had said to someone, he was more a petty annoyance than anything else. Could anyone really have hated him enough to kill him?

# Chapter Six

"Hey, Lundquist, get your phone."

Fred Lundquist smoothed his thinning blond hair, flicked a crumb from one gray lapel, and covered the distance from the coffeepot to his desk in three long strides.

"Lieutenant Lundquist."

"Fred, Sam Wade's holding for you. He's come up with a weird one. Do what you can with it—he asked for you." Captain Warren Altschuler, chief of detectives, was a realist.

Lundquist waited for the click and answered again.

"Lundquist."

"Fred, this is Sam Wade. I'd appreciate it if you'd respond to a complaint for me."

"What's up?"

"Probably nothing, but officially I'm asking you to look into a suspected homicide. George Petris died last night in emergency. You know him?"

"The Greek restaurant?"

"No, this one's a professor, but I knew him from the orchestra. He collapsed in the middle of last night's rehearsal. A couple of people took him to emergency and he died almost as soon as they got him there—the hospital says heart. One of the fellows who took him over is convinced he was poisoned with some Japanese fish. Yoichi Nakamura—our manager—very conscientious, but it sounds to me as if he's off the deep end on this one. I have to respond, though. I sat next to Petris, for Christ's sake."

"Yeah, sure, I'll check it out. You want to spell those names for me?"

Sam spelled them.

Keep the public happy for the politicians. Wade didn't think there was anything to it, but he didn't mind tying up your day proving it to a worrywart. Lundquist picked up the phone again and dialed.

"Mr. Nakamura? Detective Lieutenant Lundquist, Oliver Police Department. The prosecutor has asked me to investigate your problem. Yes. I'd like to come over to ask you some questions. Your address...? I'll be there."

He didn't hurry. The whole thing sounded like a hand-holding job, not an investigation, and it wasn't the first time he'd had that sort of call recently. At fifty, a Democratic fish in stagnant Republican waters, Fred Lundquist knew he'd never make captain, much less chief. He'd long since lost any illusions about the merit system. His outstanding record in his years of big-city experience had little to do with the realities of starting over in a place like Oliver. Party aside, being anything other than an Oliver native counted against him. If Wade really suspected a homicide, particularly one that a good detective could get credit for cracking, he'd call on a Deckard, not a Lundquist. In the near-campus traffic, he took his time and meditated on the advantages of taking an early retirement.

He could afford it. The divorce had left him remarkably unencumbered. No child support, not even alimony. She had the house....He'd probably never be able to swing a house again. If she'd stuck it out, if they'd had kids...if. He'd thought moving back to a smaller town would help, but even here she couldn't take being a cop's wife. Or could she? Maybe she just couldn't take Fred Lundquist. He wasn't all that fond of himself some days.

A lot of guys had small businesses set up, more in preparation for retirement than anything else. You could see some of them becoming more and more involved in their moonlighting—and less and less effective on the job. Burned out as he was feeling, he didn't think he could hold up his head if he let that happen. Not that he had anything to worry about. The closest thing to moonlighting he had going was the occasional sourdough he baked for Catherine's Catering. In his present mood, slapping the loaves around appealed to him in a therapeutic sort of way—but a future of nothing but baking? He shuddered.

He turned into the narrow street and swerved to avoid four Muslim girls, heads covered and long skirts swaying gracefully as they walked to class, oblivious to sidewalks and oncoming traffic. Ten years ago, he thought, a group like that would have turned heads. Now they were commonplace. Foreign oil was flooding even this small college town with new students.

Nakamura was waiting for him on the front porch of the rambling house. They passed half a dozen mailboxes by the front door and climbed two flights to an apartment carved out of an attic. At five-eleven, Lundquist could stand erect only in the center of the single room, furnished even more sparsely than his own place. Nakamura slipped out of his shoes so smoothly that Lundquist almost missed it. For a moment he considered following suit, but he repressed the impulse. Nakamura seemed not to notice. From a corner he brought a large cushion covered in rough cotton.

"Please forgive me. I almost never have visitors. If you are uncomfortable, I will be happy to borrow a chair from my neighbor. Will you have some tea with me?"

"Thank you. This is just fine." Lundquist planted both feet on the floor and leaned forward, ignoring the peculiar angle of his knees. "Suppose you tell me what happened."

"It was during the orchestra rehearsal last night," Nakamura said, kneeling on the floor, his back straight. "The first half was just a rehearsal. No problem. George—Mr. Petris—was playing very well. He usually did. I spoke to him during the break at eight-thirty and he was fine then, too. But when we started again, he couldn't play and almost dropped his instrument. A viola player drove him to the hospital and I went along to help. He died only a few moments after we arrived."

"Did a doctor see him?"

"Yes. Dr. Ito was examining him when he died."

Somewhere, a teakettle burbled and whistled.

"Excuse me, please." Nakamura rose and disappeared behind a screen.

"Did he give you an opinion about the cause of death?" Lundquist called.

"Not me." Nakamura came back carrying a round tray with a plain brown teapot and two cups without handles. Kneeling, he set the tray on the floor in front of Lundquist. "He told Daniel Petris that it was his heart."

"And you think?"

A long pause. Nakamura kept his eyes on his hands as he poured the tea.

"I don't know what to think," he said.

Lundquist inhaled the green tea, wishing it were coffee. Give me strength, he thought. Now I have to drag it out of him.

"Thank you," he said aloud. "Mr. Nakamura, you called the prosecutor's office."

"Yes."

"Why?"

The pause was even longer this time. Nakamura stared into his teacup.

"I was afraid someone had murdered him." His voice was almost inaudible.

Lundquist too spoke softly.

"What made you suspect that, Mr. Nakamura?"

Maybe it was the tea. Maybe it was the difference between "think" and "suspect." For whatever reasons, the young man stopped hesitating.

"Dr. Ito didn't see him in the orchestra. By the time he saw him, I'm sure it was his heart. But I heard a fine oboe player suddenly lose his lip and then saw him lose control over his fingers, and my assistant heard him say the word 'numb.' Then he could no longer speak at all. We had to help him to the car. He never cried out or complained of pain. He didn't hold his chest or stomach. In the car, he was scarcely breathing. By the time we arrived at the hospital, he couldn't move at all."

He paused. "I don't know how to explain it. I am not a doctor. I can only tell you that the death of George Petris was nothing like the death of my friend's mother. She died of a heart attack, and I remember it clearly. But everything that happened to George happened to my uncle, who ate a poisonous Japanese fish. It is called *fugu* in Japanese. I looked it up in my dictionary for you. You call it a puffer fish."

Something vaguely familiar nudged the back of Lundquist's mind. Where had he read about puffer fish recently?

"What did Dr. Ito say—did you tell him about your uncle?"

"He said it was possible."

"Even if Mr. Petris did die from eating this puffer fish, why would that make you suspect murder?"

"No place in Oliver serves Japanese food. His son says he ate steak last night and only fresh vegetables. If he died from this poison—or even from one of the others like it—I don't think the poison could have been in his food unless someone put it there."

"Do you know if he had any enemies?"

No answer. Nakamura poured more tea.

"Mr. Nakamura, help me. I can talk to the people you mentioned, but I might as well go home if they won't tell me what they know. You called us, remember?"

"I don't know anything. But I think that very few people liked George Petris. He was not...a courteous man."

"That's all? People don't kill people for their manners. We'd have daily slaughter on the roads if they did." He heard his own words. All too close to the truth.

"I don't think anyone would want to kill a man for the things I have seen. But I wonder if a person who is so insensitive in small matters is not also unkind in larger things. I don't know if anyone loved George. I will not be surprised to learn that someone hated him."

"Was he married?"

"I don't know. No one mentioned his wife."

"How did the son react—Daniel, did you say?"

"Yes. He said almost nothing. He didn't want to look at his father. I asked all the questions. The doctor said they would keep George's body for an autopsy because he died so suddenly. Daniel said, 'All right.' Then he left."

If it was Daniel, they were looking for a slow poison. Lundquist's legs were beginning to cramp. He tried a new position.

"What time did the rehearsal begin?"

"At seven-thirty."

"And Petris wasn't sick until after eight-thirty?"

"That's right. He even had some refreshments. I talked to him then."

"He what?"

"Oh…" The light dawned. "I didn't think of that. The orchestra has a cold drink and some cookies during the rehearsal break.

"How is that set up? Do you serve yourselves? Who provides it?"

"The women of the guild bring it in and serve it to us. Last night Mrs. Wade and Mrs. Wallston were there."

"Do you know their full names?"

"Mrs. Wade is Evelyn—Sam Wade's wife. I think it's Glenda Wallston. I don't know her husband."

"Did you see which of them served George Petris last night?"

"No."

"Who cleans up afterwards?"

"The women who serve." Nakamura returned his cup to the tray. Lundquist followed suit.

"Do you have any reason to suspect one of those women?"

"No…" It was not all convincing. Lundquist waited.

"I have no reason to suspect anyone. I only think of my uncle. He lived only a few minutes after eating that fish on the dock, instead of taking it to someone who could prepare it safely. And a few minutes after the refreshments were served, George became ill. Maybe someone else was there when he picked up his drink."

"A player?"

Nakamura sat silent, not meeting his eyes.

"Can you give me a list of the members of the orchestra?"

"Yes. I had prepared the lists to hand out last night, but I forgot to do it. They were with my violin when I picked it up this morning."

"You went back to the school?"

"No, I went to the home of Joan Spencer, my new assistant. She kept everything for me." He knelt by a small cupboard under the eaves and brought out a neat list of names, addresses, phone numbers, and instruments. "She took over after I left. She says she knew about the fish, too, from a cookbook. Her name is there with the violas. I added the address and phone of the place she works."

"Thank you. You do meet each week at the high school?"

"Yes. I assume we will rehearse next week. I don't know whether we can find another oboe by then."

Lundquist's joints creaked when he stood up.

"Thank you for your help, Mr. Nakamura. I wish I could tell you that I am sure we'll find out what happened, but I'm not. I'm certain the prosecutor will proceed if we discover anything that confirms your suspicion." Listen to me, he thought. I should go into politics myself.

On the way back down the stairs, the cooking smells of a miniature United Nations set his mouth watering. He promised himself lunch at the new Lebanese place before checking back at the station and beginning the work this nebulous investigation would involve. Hospital first, for some hard facts. Then, just in case there was anything to it, he'd better take a look at the school and pay a visit to Daniel Petris. He might talk first to the Spencer woman. She seemed to have picked up the loose ends. The school janitor would have wiped out any physical evidence, unless by some unbelievable luck the drinks had been served in glasses. Even so, they'd be clean by now, especially if one of the two who served had had it in for Petris. No longer convinced that Nakamura was making it all up, he still saw little chance of uncovering much. It was a typical Lundquist assignment, all right.

# Chapter Seven

To Joan's relief, the center had been quiet in the morning. She was grateful to sink into herself for long minutes without any need to hide her feelings. In a few minutes, she knew, the women— mostly—would arrive to open the Senior Craft Shop.

It would be an afternoon of unforced companionship with no program to push, as the knitters and quilters and crocheters plied their needles together while waiting for the few loyal customers who had discovered this inexpensive source of handmade gifts.

An hour later, the shop was in full swing. Customers were indeed scarce, but nobody seemed to mind. As she had suspected, conversation took precedence over cash. A pregnant woman buying baby booties was being instructed by the diminutive top-knotted knitter selling them. "We'll have to keep an eye on Annie," Joan teased. "She's converting the customers."

"Never you mind," said Annie. "I'd rather teach someone how to knit than sell booties any day. You find a color you like, honey, and I'll help you make a sweater and hat, too. That quaker stitch pattern 's older 'n you are. It's mighty sweet on a baby, and not a bit hard."

The young woman smiled shyly, eyes sparkling. "Would you really teach me? I bought some yarn and I've been trying, but I get it all wrong. I'd love to make something for the baby."

"'Course you would. And if you come when I'm not here, there's half a dozen others could show you."

When the mother-to-be left, Joan suddenly recognized her as the cellist who had struggled with her knitting during the orchestra rehearsal. And next through the door was Elmer Rush, pushing his granddaughter in a wheelchair. Joan greeted them warmly.

"I've been wondering when I'd see you here."

"Julie likes to come on craft shop days. She brought her newest potholders, didn't you, punkin?" He leaned down and stroked the girl's short hair.

"Oh, I'm glad. That's what I want to buy today."

Julie beamed pleasure. She held out a package of bright colors. "I make 'em."

"They're very pretty. I like the blue ones best. And the red ones. Do you have two of each?"

Julie looked at Elmer. "Here's a blue one, Julie. Now find another one just like it." To Joan he said, "She's learning colors with these things. That's why each one in this batch is all one color."

"I like them plain. It's a long hard job, isn't it, Elmer? How old is she?"

"She'll be twenty-seven next month. It's really very kind of the ladies here to let her in on their craft sales."

"I don't think they're sticklers for rules."

"A blue one!" Julie said loudly.

"Good girl. Now look for a red one. Good. And another red one."

Julie proudly held out the four potholders to Joan. "I make 'em."

"Thank you, Julie. How much do they cost?"

Julie looked at Elmer again. "Tell her a quarter, Julie." She did. Joan hunted up her purse and sorted out four quarters while Elmer settled Julie at the table. She pocketed the quarters and began almost immediately to stretch red jersey loops over the prongs of her metal loom.

"She's set for a while now," said Elmer. "She'll need help for some of the weaving, but she can do this part alone."

Already the women at the table were talking to her. Elmer turned back to Joan. "I heard on the noon news that George Petris died."

"Yoichi came to pick up his violin and he told me."

"It was so sudden."

"According to Yoichi, they barely made it to the hospital. He stopped breathing and they couldn't revive him."

"Maybe it's just as well." He looked over at Julie.

"Do you really mean that, Elmer?"

"Some days I think I do. If they'd just brought her back a little sooner. Most people either drown or are fine. But Julie…"

"How did it happen?"

"Oh, the pool hired its usual crew—good enough kids, a little whistle happy. Then this hotshot. Thought he was God's gift to women. Scrawny crew-cut kid with shoulders and a tan. He was supposed to be guarding the kiddy pool at the club where Bob—my daughter's husband—used to like to play golf. Martha would go out on the course with him and she'd have the babysitter take Julie to the pool. That day she got caught on the bottom of the pool and not a soul was paying attention."

"What about the guard and the sitter?"

"They were drinking and necking on the lifeguard's bench. Seems she'd been packing vodka in Julie's little beach bag all summer. When she'd show up, he'd volunteer for the kiddy pool. The other guards thought it was pretty boring, and they knew he had a girl, so no one checked up on him."

"Couldn't anyone see them?"

"The little pool was around the corner. That's why they needed an extra guard."

"What finally happened?"

"My wife and I drove in from Palo Alto to surprise Martha and Bob. When we found them gone, we knew where to look and I figured Julie would be at the pool. She was sweet as she is now, and sharp as a tack."

Julie, opening and closing her mouth in concentration as she struggled with the obstreperous loops, looked up suddenly, smiled at Elmer, and went back to her task.

"Couldn't they do anything for her?"

"Oh, yes. When she was in a coma for so long, one physical therapist taught us exercises to keep her muscle tone and flexibility. The woman wouldn't let us quit. Said if we did, Julie'd spend the rest of her life in bed, all twisted. She has a lot compared to that and she improves a little all the time. But it's very slow, even now."

"Will she ever walk?"

"She walks, but it's slow. The wheelchair is handy, that's all. Kind of a big stroller."

"Elmer, what happened to the lifeguard and the girl?"

"He was under eighteen. Had his hand slapped as a juvenile. They charged him with criminal negligence or whatever they call it for juveniles—I think only because of the alcohol. Lost his job, of course, and went back home on some kind of probation. The girl was eighteen. She paid a fine and served a few days."

"That's all?"

"That's all. I wonder how they live with themselves."

"Do they know?"

"They knew then. Maybe they've managed to forget." His lips tightened and the fingers of his right hand tapped a steady rhythm on his thigh. "I only wish we could."

"Maybe George *was* lucky." Maybe Ken was, too, she suddenly thought. But she instantly rejected the idea. Maybe we're all lucky not to have lived in Hiroshima, or during the Spanish Inquisition. While I'm thinking lucky, why don't I think them back alive and well, and Julie bright and active, as she would have been?

"Maybe," Elmer answered her spoken words. "But you know, I love her and I'm glad she's here, even like this. Selfish of me, isn't it?" His faded blue eyes glistened.

"She's lucky to have you, Elmer. Any girl would be." She gave him a quick hug. Not quick enough.

"Look out, look out," said Annie. "That man'll charm the socks off you and leave you checking to see if you still have ten toes."

Joan blushed. Elmer grinned at her. "No privacy around here. Peddle your knitting, Annie, and give a feller a chance."

It was a long time since anyone but Andrew had teased her. It felt good.

She didn't notice the door opening again until Annie nudged her with a knitting needle.

"There you go, Joanie. This one's more your type."

"Go on," Joan said, laughing, but a moment later she had to admire Annie's taste in Vikings. The tall man looking down at her and calling her by name had blue eyes that were anything but faded, and something about his mouth reminded her a little of Ken.

🎶

Lundquist, entering, saw a radiant woman whose warmth reached out to those around her. He had no trouble picking her out; except for the girl in the wheelchair, she was the only person in the room under sixty.

"Mrs. Spencer? Detective Lieutenant Lundquist, Oliver Police. Is there a place we could talk for a few minutes?"

"Yes, of course. Come into the office." She exchanged glances with the man next to her and patted the girl's shoulder.

He felt the eyes of all the old ladies bore into his back as he followed her to the tiny room with a desk and two chairs. She beckoned him to one that looked sturdy enough for his frame and sat down in a canvas contraption he would have been less willing to test.

"How can I help you, Lieutenant?" Wisps of dark hair had strayed from a wooden clasp to curl around her ears. Her voice and smiling eyes more than compensated for a nose with a slight but unmistakable similarity to a ski jump.

"I'm checking into the death of George Petris."

"Yoichi did go to the prosecutor, then?" she asked.

"Yes. How did you know?"

"I'm afraid I suggested it."

He waited.

"He was so upset. And he was convinced that George had died the way his uncle died—did he tell you all this?"

He nodded.

"It didn't sound very likely, but I thought maybe Sam would know what to do. I'm glad he didn't dismiss him without doing anything at all."

"No, he didn't." He dumped it in my lap, instead. "At this stage of things, I don't know what we're dealing with. I may need to talk to you again, but right now I have only a couple of questions."

"All right."

"You're Nakamura's assistant? He says you were probably one of the last people at the rehearsal."

"Yes, that's right. I was the last person there, except for Nancy Van Allen, who rode home with me, and John Hocking, who came to pick up his viola after driving George to the hospital."

"And the janitor?"

"Hadn't arrived yet."

"I'm especially interested in the refreshments that were served during the intermission. Were there any leftovers?"

"There might have been. But surely…We all had them. There was nothing fishy about them. I mean…"

"Not literally. Sure. But the preliminary medical report is not inconsistent with poisoning of some kind."

"Oh. You'd have to ask Evelyn Wade about leftovers. Or Glenda somebody. I don't know all the names yet."

"What about cups?"

"Styrofoam. They all went into the trash."

"Exactly what was served?"

"Chocolate chip cookies and something wet and horrible. Kool-Aid, maybe. It was fairly bitter both times I had it at rehearsal. I think you could put anything in it and nobody would notice."

"Do you know why anybody might want George Petris dead?"

She hesitated. "I met him only a week ago. I found him very unpleasant and I heard gossip about him that might suggest several people. He was a me-first kind of person. Somebody might have resented coming last. Even I…"

He raised his eyebrows. "Even you…?"

"Only a few minutes before he fell, I was wishing terrible things for him. It's silly, but I can't help feeling that it's all my fault." There was no smile in her eyes now.

"Did anyone like him?"

"I'm told that some women found him irresistible. And, you know, Elmer Rush and he were getting along very well last night. He's the man with the retarded grandchild over there at the crafts table. He sat behind George."

"Old friends?"

"No, Elmer is new in town. I imagine they met last week."

"You mentioned gossip."

"Nancy was telling me a rather involved story. I'd rather you asked her. I'd never get it right, even if it's true."

She looked uncomfortable. He didn't push it.

"I wonder if he didn't just get sick," she said. "People do, you know."

"It's certainly possible." I'm going through the motions to keep old Sam looking good, that's all. "By the way, Mr. Nakamura mentioned that you had a book with some information about that fish of his."

"Yes, a cookbook. Would you like me to hunt it up for you? It's still in the moving boxes."

"I'm not sure how much use it will be, but I'd appreciate it."

"That's all right. If you aren't in a hurry, though, I'll wait until Saturday to tackle those boxes."

"No hurry. It's a long shot. I'll come by your place Saturday."

She saw him to the door. He considered stopping to talk to the old man but decided he'd keep. Several faces turned blankly from the television set tuned to one of the soaps as he passed their upholstered corner. To a bridge foursome deep in a postmortem he didn't exist, but the old ladies at the crafts table, who had heard him announce himself, weren't missing a thing. Under their scrutiny he felt like a teenager on his first date.

She caught the expression on his face. "They are rather intimidating, aren't they?" She grinned. "They were giving me a hard time just before you came in. It's like having a whole crew of big sisters."

"Joanie, we're just looking out for your interests," said a plump woman behind the cash box.

"And Elmer's," another put in.

"You're terrible." She was laughing now. Not an embarrassed laugh, but a comfortable one among friends. He enjoyed watching her.

"Saturday, then," he said, deadpan. Abandoning her to them without mercy, he ducked out the door.

# Chapter Eight

The shower must be icy by now. Joan called up the stairs, knowing full well he couldn't hear her.

"Andrew, supper in five minutes."

The water stopped. ESP, maybe. She heard a muffled acknowledgment to her second call.

He appeared, shaking his wet head, puppy-like. Still barefoot, but dressed in a soft blue shirt, clean jeans, and a denim vest, he clearly had plans for the evening.

"You look reasonably spiffy."

"Clean clear through. What's for supper?" He pulled up his chair.

"Pork chops, baked potatoes, salad, and apple crisp."

"Smells great. Okay if I pass on the dessert?"

"Sure. Have it for breakfast. Why?"

"Got a date. Might need the space. You don't need the car tonight, do you?" He speared a pork chop.

"You can have it. Where are you going?"

"I'm not sure yet. I just met this girl today. I've seen her around school—she's a senior—and this afternoon she was hanging out over at the Student Union, on campus. I think her dad's a professor. Chem or bio, I'm not sure. Say, Mom, people were really talking about Mr. Petris today. You should have heard all the garbage they were saying."

"What kind of garbage?"

"Well, you know. You do know, don't you? I mean, what happened to him?"

"I know he died. I heard that this morning."

"So did everyone else. I guess it was on the radio or something. And nobody liked him. The students at the Union really hated his guts. Some girl said he committed suicide and they shouted her down—said he didn't have enough sense. Someone else said it was a student he flunked last year, getting revenge. I told them he just got sick last night and you saw it."

"That's true, Andrew, but it doesn't really tell you much. The police didn't mention suicide, but they're looking into the possibility that he was murdered. Yoichi came by this morning and told me he thought George was poisoned with a Japanese fish."

"Mom, that's crazy."

"He was very persuasive. But I think you're right."

"Wait'll they hear that."

"Not from you, I hope."

"It'll get around without me, don't worry. Gotta go. Thanks for supper. See you late—I hope." He leered at her.

"I don't promise to wait up."

"Good. New chick—no telling what time." Twirling an imaginary mustache, he flashed her an expensively straight set of teeth and took the stairs two at a time, presumably to put on his shoes. From the look of him tonight, she thought he might even tie them.

She was still clearing the dishes when Nancy phoned to propose a movie. Joan jumped at the chance. She didn't want to spend this particular evening at home alone. When she got into Nancy's car, however, she found she wouldn't escape so easily.

"Joan, I couldn't believe it when I heard it on the radio!" Nancy greeted her, starting up with only one eye on the road. "I called Yoichi and he said it was all true."

"What was?"

"The radio said George died of unknown causes, but Yoichi said he thought it was murder, and that you told him to call the police."

"Not exactly. He felt terrible and I suggested that Sam might look into it for him."

"But the police talked to him. And he said he mentioned you. Did they come to you, too?"

"Well, yes."

"You see? And they'll probably talk to Daniel. They always check on the family first. I wouldn't blame that boy if he did kill his father. In fact, it wouldn't be hard to blame anyone for doing George in."

"Nancy!"

"You didn't know him. I told you how he took over Daniel's girlfriend, Lisa Wallston, and then dumped her flat. Did you realize that Lisa's mother served the punch last night?"

"She did what?" Joan asked weakly, having heard it clearly the first time.

"She was handing out the punch. She and Evelyn. Don't you remember? When Alex asked who knew Daniel—to call him—someone had the nerve to suggest Glenda Wallston. Talk about tactless."

"Do you think she poisoned George's punch?"

"Heavens, I don't know. But she'd probably know how. She's a nurse, you know."

"No, I—"

"Yes. She works at the hospital—in OB, I think—but surely anyone over there could find out enough about poison to kill a man. And if there ever was a person who had reason to, Glenda's the one. Lisa isn't twenty-one yet, but the rumors flying around town have shot her reputation. I've heard she was sleeping with George and Daniel at the same time, that she was pregnant and had an abortion, that she didn't have an abortion and gave up the baby for adoption because her mother wouldn't let her bring it home. Even that she's become a lesbian. You name it, somebody's said it about Lisa."

"You think gossip would make Glenda kill George?"

"Gossip—and ruining her daughter's life. Of course, it might not be Glenda. There's Daniel. Poor Daniel. His father gave him enough grief before all that."

"He did?" More and more, she was regretting having mentioned Nancy and her gossip to Lieutenant Lundquist.

"George was such a snob. Wouldn't you know he'd have a son whose ambition is to work with his hands. Daniel is a marvel with wood, but you'd never catch George recognizing anything but abstract academic ability. I think he looked down on engineers as mere technicians. Daniel can't even have a shop at home. He has to sneak off to Isaac, the violin maker. I've seen him at the shop when I've done ads for it, and it looks to me as if he's quietly apprenticed himself to Isaac. It's the only place I've ever seen him look happy. You'd think a man would be proud to have a future Stradivarius for a son, but not George. I'll bet he never knew what Daniel was up to, or he would have managed to stop it somehow. Well, he can't stop it now."

"Look, Nancy, someone's pulling out of that space. Is it big enough?" To Joan's relief, Nancy shifted her attention to the trick of parking a large car in a short parallel spot between two small ones. The movie that had seemed a welcome diversion failed to hold Joan's attention. When they left the theater, she couldn't have described the plot, but she was grateful that Nancy chose to dissect it on the way home. An occasional "uh-huh" was all that was required of her.

The light in Andrew's window surprised her.

"Nancy, I'd ask you in, but Andrew's home. I didn't expect him so early. I'd better see if he's all right."

If Nancy saw through the deception, she put a good face on it. Upstairs, Joan called to Andrew, heard him answer, and fell asleep in less time than she would have thought possible.

It was morning before she learned why he had come home so soon. He leaned against the refrigerator and watched her wash up after breakfast.

"I thought I had a date, but it sure wasn't much. We took a walk and she let me buy her an egg roll at Liu's Place. Then she asked me to give her dad a ride home from work."

"Night shift?" She tried to remember what he'd said about the girl.

"No, he's a biology professor. We picked him up at his lab. Actually, it was pretty interesting. He showed us around and talked about what he was doing. Maybe that's why Jennifer wanted me to go there. She's a funny girl."

"Should I ask?"

"Not weird, Mom, just hard to figure out. I mean, going to her dad's lab to get rid of a date is a little extreme. All she had to do was say she wanted to go home."

"Maybe her dad needed a ride."

"Maybe, but this isn't the first time."

"I thought you just met her."

"I did, but she told me she takes guys there all the time. I think she likes to show him off. She took Daniel Petris there on a date, too. She was talking about him some. She didn't think he'd be all that broken up about his dad."

"No one seems to be." She drained the sink.

"Jennifer sure wasn't. She plays oboe. I mean, she's serious about it. She says that when the symphony's youth concerto competitions came around, Petris always judged woodwinds. He didn't criticize her technique—I guess she's so good you couldn't—but he marked her way low on her tone and said she was unmusical, whatever that means. The other two judges told her they liked her, but she's lost two years in a row, even though there was only one of him and two of them. She was afraid she wouldn't get into music school if she couldn't win again this year. She's really relieved."

Joan took a deep breath. "I think if I hear one more person isn't sorry he died, I'll...I don't know what. Let's change the subject, okay? Tell me about the lab."

"Sure. You're not squeamish about frogs, are you, Mom?"

"Frogs? No I think you're safe."

"Well, Mr. Werner's doing an experiment on how their olfactory bulb works—that's the part of their brain in charge of smelling. He has tubes hooked up to jars full of smells, and he puffs air on what looks like the frog's nostrils—it's really the olfactory epithelium. Then he measures the frog's reaction."

"And the frog just sits there and lets him do that?"

"The frog doesn't have any choice. Before he starts the experiment—this is why I asked how you felt about frogs—he destroys its brain and its spinal cord. It can't move. It can't feel anything, either. It's like brain death. It's really a dead frog."

"Then how can it be smelling?"

"It isn't, exactly. Not the way a live frog does. Its olfactory bulb is separate from the rest of its brain—that's why he chose frogs—and that bulb is still hooked up to the frog's face, where the airs puffs hit. Mr. Werner is studying a certain kind of nerve cell that way. He uses a nerve poison called TTX to block out the impulses from the other nerve cells and leave him with just the kind he wants to study. It's really interesting."

"I didn't know you were interested in that sort of thing."

"Neither did I, until I started telling you about it. That's funny."

"You didn't like biology that much when you took it, did you?"

"It was so dead. What I like is that he doesn't know how it's going to come out. And he says it could help us understand how nervous systems process information. That could be really important."

She couldn't remember this long a speech from Andrew in months. His eyes were alight, and he was running his hands through his hair as he talked, an old habit of his father's.

"Does he use student assistants?"

"In the lab? I don't know. I bet he doesn't hire them, because he was talking about all kinds of places he cuts corners to save money. Oliver doesn't exactly have a big research budget." He paused and said slowly, "I wonder if he'd let me work for him for free."

"Maybe it wasn't a wasted date after all."

"Maybe. And maybe if I worked in the lab, Jennifer would go out with me on a real one sometime. He probably stakes her out in the Union as bait to trap him a stable of lab assistants."

"You have a conniving mind. That doesn't mean *he* does."

"He connived enough to get himself written up in the paper. Big feature story. Jennifer framed the article and hung it on the wall. I think it embarrassed him, though."

"What's he like as a person?"

"Not bad. You could tell he was excited about what he was doing, but he didn't push it down your throat. He has a sense of humor, too. He showed us a couple of puffs on the frog he was finishing up, and when he packed up for the night and put the dead frog in the freezer, he said he hated to waste good frog's legs but he didn't want to do us in. That TTX is really powerful stuff. Maybe someone fed Petris a used frog's leg or two."

"Andrew!"

"Sorry, Mom. That wasn't funny. And he didn't say it. But you know, someone could have. Done it, I mean. Anyone could walk in there. The building was open when we got there at nine. His lab was unlocked, too. He was down the hall, and Jennifer just marched me upstairs and into the lab to wait for him. The whole town would know about the TTX. It was in that big article about him last year."

"Lots of people have poisons."

"I guess so. See you tonight, Mom. I'll be home for supper and I don't have a date. Jennifer can snare another guy for her dad tonight."

# Chapter Nine

Thursday's paper had reported the sudden death of Professor George Petris. His obituary mentioned his novel—starting a minor flurry in both local bookstores (which hadn't sold a copy for months), his temporary deanship half a dozen years before (the scars of which were just beginning to heal), and his membership in the First Methodist Church (which came as a surprise to a number of active Methodists). He was, it said, survived by one son, Daniel, of Oliver, and a daughter, Emily, of San Jose, California. Arrangements were pending at Snarr's Funeral Home.

By the time Friday's paper announced that the police were investigating the matter, most residents of Oliver already thought they knew more than the meager story told. Well acquainted with the crop of wagging tongues, Lundquist cultivated it for the occasional grain of truth among the chaff. He spent Friday morning answering and returning telephone calls from people who thought they could set the police straight.

Most were complaints about the murdered man and generous hints about other people who would be glad to have seen the last of him. He heard a number of versions of the story about Lisa Wallston and her relationships with the Petris men. A woman who sang in the church choir with Glenda accused her of keeping up her membership as a blind to conceal her murderous inclinations. An orchestra member who had heard the poison story was certain Evelyn Wade must have dropped something in Petris's punch to get first chair for Sam. Sure.

Then he heard from Harold Williams. Williams wasn't blaming anyone in particular.

"There was no love lost between us, but I didn't kill him, and if someone did, I don't want him to get away with it. Is it true that he was poisoned?"

"It's possible."

"I've been talking with Yoichi Nakamura. I run Aqua Heaven, the aquarium shop on North Rogers. We don't have any puffer fish, but we do carry a salamander that contains the same poison. Actually, there are quite a few varieties of fish like that, but the Japanese puffer fish and our California salamanders share exactly the same poison. And I know it's deadly."

"Are you suggesting that someone used your salamanders?"

"It could be done."

"Have you sold any recently?"

"Not many. Lisa Wallston came in a week or so ago and replaced her whole aquarium. Something had fouled the water and killed everything. She must have bought a dozen."

"Oh?"

"Of course, it's not very likely someone would do that, not when the straight poison is available."

"The straight poison?"

"Well, sure. Over at the college. That's the stuff Carl Werner is using in his experiments. There was a big thing in the paper about it last spring. That's where I learned that the puffer fish poison and the poison in my salamanders was the same."

Lundquist nodded. He'd remembered all along that he'd read something about puffer fish.

"Mr. Williams, you've been very helpful. I appreciate your call."

"No trouble. Just hope you catch up with whoever did it."

He sat for a moment, chewing his lip. Then he picked up the phone again and quickly confirmed what he'd begun to suspect. As he already knew, the preliminary autopsy results on Petris had showed nothing inconsistent with poisoning, but there had been no fish in the contents of his stomach and no trace of any poison. There were some signs of coronary artery disease. Heart attack was still the best guess. In the absence of Nakamura's insistence, it would have been the only guess. The pathologist knew the poison in the fish. In its pure form the stuff was so lethal—more than a thousand times as toxic as arsenic, about a hundred times as deadly as curare—that the tiny amount needed to kill might very well all be metabolized in the short time before the victim died. Yes, he would try sending to a special lab for the toxicology, but it was a long shot. Gas chromatography and mass spectrometry might have a chance of finding something.

"Don't hold your breath," the pathologist warned. "You may not get the report for a couple of months."

Lundquist leaned back in his swivel chair, anchoring his toes under a desk drawer against its tendency to tilt unexpectedly. He had no more real evidence than before and from the sound of it, he wasn't likely to get any. In his heart of hearts, however, he'd just switched from a case of political babysitting to a homicide investigation. But for the coincidence of Nakamura's uncle, no one would even be doing the babysitting. Petris would simply have died, and from what he'd learned so far, no one would have mourned him.

How did you go back to the mother and tell her the baby had just passed puberty while in your care? And become impossible in the process, Lundquist thought wryly. It was all very well to make Wade look good with an investigation after which he could report to all the good citizens that no murder had existed and they were safe in their beds. He wouldn't welcome a real murder he didn't have the first chance of clearing up.

Lundquist had no desire to face the prosecutor with his suspicion. Or his own supervisor of detectives, for that matter. He knew what they'd say about hunches. He could wait. The murderer (if there was one, he reminded himself) should be feeling safe. Anybody who knew enough to use that stuff must know enough not to expect it to be traced. Or would he? If the whole town knew about Werner's lab, the murderer might not be an expert. He needed to see that article. Bob Peterson at the *Courier* would dig it up for him. Bob owed him for a story or two.

♮♮♮

Daniel Petris met him at the door and took him down the hallway of a house that seemed to be insulated with books, past a door through which he glimpsed a desk his former wife would have itched to straighten.

Lundquist saw no flowers, smelled no baked meats, met no relatives.

They sat opposite each other in massive leather chairs before the cold fireplace in the living room, lined with books as the hall and study had been. Not the matched sets of a decorator, but the hodgepodge of a real reader. A slender young man not more than five-seven, Daniel was almost swallowed up in the upholstery. His calloused fingers were bitten to the quick and he nibbled at the sides of a thumb.

"I'm sorry to intrude," Lundquist said formally. "I was hoping you could help me with a few questions about your father."

"Like what?"

"The hospital told me that he had no personal physician. I wondered if that was correct, or if he was simply unable to tell them anything."

"It's probably true. The only time I remember hearing him mention a doctor, he called them all quacks. He never got sick and he had very little patience with people who did."

"So you wouldn't know whether he had a history of heart problems?"

"I never heard about any. He was big on aerobic exercise. Most mornings he'd either swim or run."

"Did he seem his normal self that evening, before the rehearsal? I understand you ate together."

"Yes. Look, I don't understand why you're here. Do the police always come when someone dies?"

"Not always. But we do when we're not sure what happened."

"Wasn't it his heart?"

"It looks that way. The doctor hasn't signed the death certificate yet, though. In cases of sudden death, it's good procedure to rule out other possibilities."

"That's what they told me when they said there would be an autopsy. Isn't that enough?"

"Sometimes."

"Is that all you want to know from me?" Daniel started on the other thumb.

"Not quite. I suppose I'm looking for some idea of the kind of man your father was."

"Oh, a great man. Just ask him," Daniel shot back and then caught himself. "Oh, God, how could I say that?"

"You didn't get along too well, is that it?"

"What are you doing? Aren't you supposed to read me my rights or something?" He stood up, clenching his bitten thumbs.

"No, you're not a suspect. At the moment nobody is. We're not even sure there's anything to suspect anybody of. People do die suddenly."

"And now you want to see how sorry I am."

"And now I want to learn anything I can that will help me find out who might have deprived you of a father."

Daniel sat down slowly. In the depths of the chair, he seemed smaller again. "I didn't kill him. But if someone else did, he didn't deprive me of a father. That happened a long time ago."

Lundquist leaned forward. "Do you want to tell me about it, son?" he asked.

"There's nothing to tell. It wasn't something that happened. It was what didn't happen. I didn't turn out to be the literary genius my father expected any son of his to be, that's all. He never knew me at all. I learned to keep out of his way and let him think what he wanted to think."

"And your mother?"

"That's really ancient history."

"Is she living?"

"Oh, she's alive, all right. She went back home, where she grew up. Took my sister with her. But I had to stay here."

"Why was that?"

"I think she was afraid I'd turn out like him. She didn't discuss it. She just left."

"How old were you?"

"When she left? Fifteen. Just finishing my first year of high school."

"Were you like your father at that age?"

"Dad would never talk much about his teens. Neither would she—she knew him then, though. I know what he thought of *me* at that age. I wasn't a real guy, because I didn't have lots of girls hanging around all the time. I wasn't a real brain, because I didn't read all the books he did. And he knew I'd never swim to Catalina Island. Can you believe it? He even did that."

"Do you still hear from your mother?"

"When she thinks of it."

"Now?"

"We talked on the phone. I told her I'd be all right. She didn't offer to come."

Lundquist heard the unshed tears. He changed the subject.

"Will you stay on here?"

"Where would I go?" Daniel's surprise appeared genuine. "You mean the house? I guess so. I mean, I think it's paid for. I don't really know. I haven't even started looking for papers and things. Dad's lawyer called. I'm supposed to talk with him on Monday. I'll stay in town, if that's what you're worried about. In spite of what my father thought, I'm learning a lot here. And I have a job. I can support myself."

"You're free to go anywhere," Lundquist assured him. "If you have any reason to leave town, though, I'd appreciate it if you'd leave word, in case we need to reach you." He paused. "There is one other thing you might be able to tell me."

Daniel waited.

"I take it your parents were divorced."

A nod.

"What kind of social life did your father have?"

"You mean women?"

"That's what I'm asking."

"He wasn't gay, if that's what you're after." Daniel bristled.

"Simmer down, son. It's been what—six or seven years since your mother left? And you said something earlier that made me think your father was interested in lots of girls when he was younger."

"He didn't change." There was no mistaking the bitterness in the young man's voice. "That's why my mother got out." He looked Lundquist in the eye. "Are you just fishing, or do you know something?"

"No, I don't know anything. But people do talk, don't they?"

"And some bigmouth told you my father stole my girl." His voice was dead now and he stared at the floor.

"Something like that."

"Well, it's true. And then he dumped her for the next good-looking woman who came along. I don't know how many he's had since then. If you think I killed him for that, I can't stop you. But I didn't." Slumped in the big chair, he didn't move.

"Did he have any enemies that you know of?"

"I think he collected them. But I never heard of anyone who hated him that much."

"Do you know if he left a will?"

"No. I guess the lawyer will tell me on Monday."

Lundquist took the names and addresses of his mother, sister, and lawyer, thanked him, and left. The kid was hurting, no question about that. Rejected by both parents—and the business about the girl—no wonder. Grief? Maybe. But for what? Guilt? Possibly. Daniel had plenty of reason to hate his father, and they had eaten together that night. He could write up those facts into a pretty damning set of circumstances, but how could he write up his gut feeling about this boy? One hunch deserves another, he decided, and reported back to the station determined not to write anything.

On his desk was a photocopy of the *Courier* story about Professor Werner and his experiments. Good. It would have to wait, though. He was due in court in half an hour to testify on a burglary case so old that he'd need at least that long to knock the cobwebs off his memory. He slid the story into the Petris file. With luck, he might be able to see the professor before he left the laboratory. Come to think of it, that probably wouldn't be too hard. Some of those publish-or-perish guys worked all hours.

He did put in a quick call to the prosecutor, telling him the preliminary investigation was inconclusive, but he'd keep him posted if anything turned up.

"Maybe when we get the results of those tests..."

"Sure, Fred, you let me know. I'll tell Nakamura we're working on it."

All of us, Lundquist thought.

"You do that, Sam."

# Chapter Ten

Standing ajar, the laboratory door was covered with cartoons. Frank and Ernest predominated, in white lab coats and frazzled hair. Lundquist knocked without reading them—a test of willpower.

"She's here, Daddy," a girl's voice called, and the door flew open.

"Oh, I was expecting someone else," said a slender blond girl of about sixteen in T-shirt, shorts, and sneakers. "Did you want my father?"

"I'm looking for Professor Werner."

"That's me." Somewhat stooped, casually shaven, Werner wore no white coat. His work pants and bulging pockets suggested an electrician, missing only the tool belt. "What can I do for you?" he asked.

The girl draped herself around a chair and assumed a look of boredom. She wouldn't miss a word.

"Detective Lieutenant Lundquist, Oliver Police. I'd appreciate a few minutes of your time."

"Come in. Jennifer, get your things together."

She unwrapped herself from the chair in slow motion and began searching the scratched desks, tables, and chairs that gave the laboratory the appearance of a garage sale. Electronic gadgets covered many tables and wires dangled from others on shelves.

Werner led Lundquist past a screened cubicle and a little jungle of plastic and glass tubing to a dingy corner with two chairs, one a sturdy kitchen castoff, the other a secretarial model with wheels.

"Sit down, please, and tell me what's up."

"That's just it. I'm not sure anything is. I've heard something about the research you're doing and need to understand it a little better. It may tie in to an investigation."

"What do you want to know?"

"I hear it has something to do with Japanese fish."

"You must have the wrong man. I use frogs."

"Didn't the newspaper article last year mention puffer fish?"

"Oh, that. Probably. But it's pretty remote."

"Suppose you tell me what you do."

"Well, there are some local circuits in the nervous system that get very little attention. The little we know about them is pretty interesting, but they're hard to study. That's where the puffer fish would come in."

"How's that?"

"It's one of the sources of a substance that blocks the transmission of nerve impulses. The stuff is called tetrodotoxin—TTX for short. It gives me a crack at the signals I want to record."

"How can it help you, if it blocks the impulses?"

"That's just it. The microcircuits I'm looking for activate other cells by graded electrical signals, not by impulses. So you see, blocking the impulses of the long cells unclutters things and leaves me with just what I want."

"I'll take your word for it. You feed the TTX to the frog?"

"No, I use it on the olfactory bulb. The microcircuits have been studied in the eye with TTX. Mudpuppy retina, usually. I'm following up on that work in another sensory system. The principle ought to be the same. I compare the electrical responses to odor with and without the TTX. We know quite a lot about the frog's sense of smell and it's fairly easy to get well-controlled stimuli. Here, have a whiff."

He reached up, unhooked a bottle from the tangle of tubing, and removed the stopper.

Lundquist didn't need to sniff. The powerful odor of rotting flesh reached him quickly.

"Daddy!"

"Sorry, Jennifer. That was putrescine. Here's amyl acetate."

A sharp, penetrating chemical smell was a clear contrast.

"If I could afford it, I'd have a tank of compressed air here, but I make do with an electric aquarium pump. Hang on while I turn on the exhaust to get rid of the stink. A charcoal filter in the tubing does it for the frog."

Breathing comfortably again, Lundquist decided it was time to cut the lecture short.

"I gather the TTX is poisonous."

"Sure is. Blocking those nerve impulses may be good for my experimental purposes, but it's no way to go on living."

"Do you prepare it yourself from the puffer fish?"

"No, it's commercially available now."

"Where do you get it?"

"Swann's Biological Supply, in Chicago."

"Can you show me what it looks like?"

"Sure." Crossing the room, Werner reached for a wire key ring hanging from a nail on a wooden cabinet. Dangling from the ring was a Hills Brothers coffee can. "An old student got tired of my losing my keys," he said over his shoulder. Unlocking the cabinet, he took out a slip of paper and bent to a padlock on a small refrigerator.

High heels clicked on the smooth lab floor.

"Jennifer, are you ready?"

Startled, Lundquist recognized Evelyn Wade in an off-the-shoulder job and fragile-looking sandals that showed her slender feet and ankles to best advantage. When he stood to greet her, he saw Sam behind her in an ordinary suit, looking rumpled by comparison.

"I'll be right there, Mrs. Wade. I just have to find my history book. It was right here a minute ago." Jennifer put her book bag down and disappeared into a back room.

"Hurry, please. We're running late as it is. I don't like to leave the children alone, but I had to pick Mr. Wade up at work tonight. His Mercedes is in the shop. Carl, how are you?" The big police lieutenant was invisible to her.

"Surviving." Werner smiled warmly at her, a small bottle in his hand.

"You driven men. Just like Sam. He was working until seven tonight, and he'll hardly have time to bathe and change for the

Bryans' dinner. Frank Bryan has decided to endorse Sam for the nomination, you know. It's just a matter of timing."

Sam nodded quietly at Lundquist. "Fred."

"Sam."

"Making any progress?"

"Too soon to tell. Professor Werner is helping me on some background."

"Thanks. I'm afraid I'm in for a long evening. I appreciate it."

"Sure."

Jennifer emerged and they left.

There were worse things than being divorced, Fred reflected. Sam didn't give the impression of an unhappy man, though. He looked at Evelyn the way most men look at women they haven't married yet. She didn't appeal to Fred. He'd like at least to be in charge of himself, he thought, if not of the whole family.

The door opened again and a curly head poked around it.

"Hi, Mr. Werner. Oh, I'm sorry. You're busy."

"It's all right, Andrew, but Jennifer just left on a baby-sitting job."

"I was really hoping to see you." He came in. "Ever since Jennifer brought me to the lab last night, I've been wondering if I could help you out sometime and learn more about what you're doing. You wouldn't have to pay me."

Werner's slow smile broke through. "I like the price. Sure, Andrew, I'd be glad to have you. When can you start?"

"Any time. Now, if you want."

"Fine. You could start by unpacking that box. I think everything in it belongs in that cabinet. You'll see how it's organized. Oh, and put this combination on the top shelf." He handed him the combination and the keys. "Hang the keys on that nail when you're done, would you?"

He showed Lundquist the small brown bottle, clearly labeled TTX—POISON.

"Here's the tetrodotoxin. It comes as a powder. I dissolve it only as I need it."

"How much would it take to kill a man?"

"About what you could put on a pinhead, maybe a little more."

Lundquist watched the boy stocking the supply cabinet.

"How many people have access to this laboratory?"

"We're pretty open. I've had very little pilferage—mostly the ballpoint pen variety. The M.D.s have more drug problems, and if you're looking for local sources of poison, I think you'd do better at Oliver Hardware or the Garden Center. That's why I lock the TTX, though. I'd hate to have someone come looking for a high and wind up dead."

"Is the laboratory door locked when no one is working here?"

"I lock up when I go home at night. Not when I'm in and out."

"Who might come in?"

"Any of my departmental colleagues. Jennifer shows up after school or in the evening, sometimes with a friend, like Andrew here. Students, of course. And anybody looking for one of us." He returned the TTX to the safe. "Don't you think it's about time you told me what you're after?"

"You've been very patient, Dr. Werner. If you could just answer one more question first."

"What is it?"

"To your knowledge, has anyone on this list ever visited the laboratory?" He handed him the orchestra personnel list prepared by Yoichi Nakamura.

Werner perched on the edge of a table and studied the list.

"I don't know a lot of these folks. Some may be students. The Wades you just saw here—Jennifer babysits for them on a fairly regular basis. Harold Williams brought the air pump in person and helped me fix it up. That's all I can recognize, but now I know why you're here. It's about George Petris, isn't it? Jennifer was spouting some nonsense about poison."

"Afraid so. Only it's a little more specific than that, if there's anything to it at all."

"What's that supposed to mean?"

"There's a possibility that it was the puffer fish poison. We have to check. This is a list of people who were with Petris the night he died."

Werner sat with his head bowed.

"It's possible," he said finally. "I don't keep close tabs on the TTX. I'd never miss the little it would take to kill a man. Anyone could have taken some. George was a difficult man, but I'll have a hard time forgiving myself if my carelessness led to his death."

"Let's not borrow trouble. So far we have no medical confirmation."

Werner couldn't look at him.

"That still won't mean it didn't happen. I'll change the lock tomorrow and keep the lab locked from now on when I so much as go across the hall." His shoulders stooped even more.

"I think that's wise. And if you think of anyone else who had access to the poison. I'd appreciate a call."

"I suppose Daniel did." The words came slowly, unwillingly.

"His son?"

"Yes, a couple of times recently he's stopped by with Jennifer after an egg roll. She eats those things like candy."

A strange sound came from behind the cabinet door.

"You all right, Andrew?" Werner asked.

"Uh, sure, I'm fine." Slow in coming, the reply was oddly muffled.

"One last question," Lundquist said. "Do you know a young woman named Lisa Wallston, or her family?"

"Never heard of them."

"Thank you. You've been very helpful."

On the way home, he mulled it over. The lab had been wide open. Any disgruntled student or faculty member—he didn't doubt that there had been both—would have had easy access to the TTX. Williams and Wade were hardly a surprise. In a town the size of Oliver the greater surprise would have been if no one from an orchestra of fifty or sixty people had been among Werner's acquaintances. Williams had, after all, told him about Werner. Sam must have read the article, too, though without the particular interest it would have had for an aquarium expert.

Then there was Daniel. He'd have to keep an open mind about Daniel. And about Werner. Most forthcoming with information that he must have known was leading to questions about the poison. Jennifer he could surely dismiss. What possible reason could she have to do in an English professor? On the other hand, if the stories he'd been hearing about Petris were true, and Daniel had confirmed them at least in part, then even Jennifer could have been entangled in his life. She had dated his son, if you could call egg rolls dates. And Werner might not be so unworldly as all that. He, too, could be concerned about his daughter, once she became even remotely involved with the Petris men. She seemed young for Daniel.

Lundquist trudged upstairs to his sterile rooms, remembering only after releasing his tired feet from their leather prisons that he had promised Catherine sourdough bread for a large party she was catering Saturday night. He retrieved the starter from its covered dish at the back of the refrigerator, divided it into two bowls, and added flour, water, and a spoonful of sugar to activate the culture. Gluten flour in one and rye in the other. If she wanted variety, he'd give it to her. Covering the lumpy messes, he cleared his mind.

Five minutes later, he slept.

# Chapter Eleven

Saturday began peacefully enough. Having luxuriated in bed until half past nine, Joan woke to bright sunshine streaming through the window. She pulled on jeans and a sweatshirt, made a pot of coffee, and threw a batch of popovers into the oven. If that didn't lure Andrew out of bed, nothing would.

Her own mouth watering at the delicious odor beginning to waft out of the kitchen, Joan parked her coffee mug on the fraying rug and attacked the dusty boxes of books. Their little house, long rented to students, was in many ways spartan, but it did feature built-in bookshelves in abundance.

Leaving a spot near the kitchen for cookbooks, she filled the shelves at one end of the old sofa with the art books Aunt Margit always sent for birthdays and Christmas. Klee and Miro flanked Lautrec and Leonardo. She sat back on her heels and debated that. Maybe Lautrec should be filed under T. Another day.

Shakespeare, the boxed set of the Greeks she'd always meant to read, well-thumbed volumes of Frost and Mörike, Sandburg's Lincoln books and the *Rutabaga Stories*, and Conan Doyle hobnobbed with Schweitzer's *Quest for the Historical Jesus* at the other end. She kicked herself for not having organized the books in her leisurely, unemployed days. Filled with new resolve, she closed the lid firmly on a box of childhood favorites. Where were the cookbooks?

She had just found them when Andrew came down the stairs barefoot, tying his robe and twitching his nose.

"Tell me, am I dreaming, or did I die and go to heaven?"

"Cute. Set the table, would you, Andrew? I'm all dusty and breakfast is about ready."

The doorbell sent him scuttling upstairs.

It was Lieutenant Lundquist in a checked flannel shirt with the sleeves rolled up, looking much less official than he had on his visit to the center.

"Come in, won't you?" Joan called to him through the screen. "Don't mind the boxes. There must be an empty chair around here somewhere." Bent double, she waved in the general direction of one.

The travel alarm she used as a timer shrilled as he shut the door.

"Oh, no! It's ten-thirty. That's the popovers and I haven't even washed my hands."

"May I take them out for you?" he offered. "When popovers are ready, they can't wait."

A cook? She wouldn't have guessed it. Come on, Sherlock, she told herself. Fine detective you'd make. There's flour all down the sides of his pants.

"Thanks, you sure could. Won't you have some with us?"

"I'll never say no."

She watched him out of the corner of her eye while scrubbing her hands and setting three places. He flipped the popovers into the waiting basket without tearing even one.

They were on their seconds when Andrew joined them, fully dressed. Hair combed, too, she noticed.

"This is my son Andrew. Andrew, this is Lieutenant Lundquist. He's trying to find out what happened to George Petris."

"Hello," said Andrew around a steaming bite. "Didn't I see you in Mr. Werner's lab last night?"

"That's right," Lundquist answered. "You came to volunteer. How was it?"

"Boring at first. I just put away supplies. But then he let me photograph some of the signals he was picking up and he explained what he thinks they mean."

"I didn't know you'd met, Lieutenant," Joan said.

"My name is Fred," Lundquist told her. "I'd feel better if you'd use it."

"All right, Fred. I'm Joan." He had nice eyes, she thought. Butter leaked down her chin to rob her of any last remnants of dignity and she discovered she didn't care.

"Have some of Annie Morrison's strawberry preserves," she said. "Remember the little old lady at the center who gave you the gimlet eye?"

"I remember a whole row of them. Did they rib you when I left?" He had the grace to sound ashamed, but a twinkle gave him away.

"You did that on purpose!"

Andrew sat mystified. She let him wonder. Comfortable now, she asked Fred how he had learned about baking.

"This kind I saw at home. But my dad was a baker, years ago. I used to watch him. For a long time, I knew I wanted to be a baker like my father. Then I got hooked on police work and now baking's just a hobby."

"You're doing it today, aren't you?" she asked.

No Watson, he looked at his pants and nodded. "I'm making some sourdough for a friend's catering service."

"That sounds like more than a hobby."

"It's just to help her out." Her. Wouldn't you know it?

"Excuse me, please. I think I'll go find that book." She wiped her fingers on the seat of her pants.

"Don't mind us," said Andrew. "Want the last one?" He offered Lundquist the basket.

"Thanks, you keep it. I'm one ahead of you. Besides, that bread's been rising for hours in this heat. I'll get what I came for and take off."

He was halfway to the living room before Andrew spoke. "My name is Fred" had clearly not been aimed at him, but "Lieutenant Lundquist" was too formal for his taste. Andrew compromised.

"Uh, Mr. Lundquist, can I ask you what you've found out about Mr. Petris? The students have some wild ideas."

"What have you heard?" The big man stopped.

"Oh, just talk." Andrew backed off. "Nothing, really."

"You tell anybody who thinks he knows something to call the station. They know how to reach me even when I'm off duty."

On cue, the telephone rang. Andrew picked it up.

"Yes, he's here." Handing over the receiver, he eavesdropped openly.

"Lundquist." He listened, the nice eyes suddenly cold, and looked at his watch. "Give me the address." He pulled a notebook from his back pocket. "One twenty-five North Merrifield. Right. I got that. I'm on my way."

He looked at their faces.

"You might as well know. Daniel Petris says he's found a dead woman. Was Wanda Borowski in the orchestra?"

Joan handed him the Time-Life *Cooking of Japan*—she'd finally found it—as if it contained eggshells.

"A Wanda sat next to George," she said. "A flutist. She packed up his oboe."

He nodded.

"You're sure she's dead?" She couldn't help asking, but in the pit of her stomach she knew.

"Sounds like it." He watched her closely. "He says her throat was cut."

Joan conquered her rising gorge. "If I can help…"

He thanked her for everything and left, not hurrying, but wasting no motion.

𝄞𝄞𝄞

The offer to help had been automatic. The phone call some ten minutes later was not.

"Joan, this is Fred Lundquist. I have an awkward kind of favor to ask."

"Yes?"

"I'm at the Borowskis' and we're short-handed. Her kids may come home any minute, but we haven't been able to reach their father. I want them out of all this."

"Was she really…?"

"Yes. She's dead, and it's messy. If the neighbors were a little younger, I'd turn to them, but they're on the trembly side. Look, it's all right. I can send them to the station."

"No, don't." Andrew had been awed by the rescue squad that failed to save his father, but she remembered how tightly his hand had clung to hers, even while he tried to comfort her. "I'll come."

# Chapter Twelve

She made it in five minutes. A small crowd had already gathered, attracted by the ambulance and the police cars, their lights flashing and radios clearly audible half a block away.

In this part of town, mostly rentals, there were no bossy neighbors plunging in to take over. Most of the onlookers stood in clumps across the street, talking among themselves, but the kids had no such restraint. Joan feared for Wanda's small but immaculate lawn. She carefully followed the curving path past a pair of limestone cubes balanced on their corners, up to the shaded front porch, where she gave her name to a uniformed man. Feeling like a goldfish in a bowl, she sat on the porch swing, her toes touching the floor, and avoided curious eyes by staring up at the spider plant and strawberry begonia that hung in pots from the porch roof. Not macramé, but some kind of crocheted holders supported them.

Lundquist didn't keep her waiting long. He led her into the living room—what her grandmother would have called the parlor. The contrast with the mess she had left at home overwhelmed her. The room smelled of furniture polish and scented candles. Fragile knickknacks and African violets crowded together on small tables, and Joan marveled at starched doilies. One overstuffed chair even wore an anti-macassar. She had stepped into another world. Yet Wanda had been a young woman. She had found time to play the flute, competently enough to hold first chair. No sloppiness anywhere. Joan wondered about the children. Were they allowed to live in this house?

"They haven't dusted in here," Fred was saying. "Can I trust you not to touch anything?"

Best-dusted room I've seen in years, she thought. But he meant the police, didn't he? Their kind of dusting would turn this fussy perfection into a nightmare for the woman who had created it. Joan reminded herself that Wanda would never know. She nodded mutely.

"If you don't mind listening," he said, "I think I'll bring Daniel in here to talk."

She wondered why he trusted her. It didn't seem very professional of him. Or did he?

"Are you sure you want me to hear it?" she asked.

"Yes. You might catch something I don't. This could tie in to his father and the orchestra."

"Then doesn't that make us all suspect?" There. She'd said it aloud.

"Not you." He smiled. "Wanda spoke to the two old ladies next door when she sent her children off to the park at ten-thirty this morning. They're sure of the time. They missed the beginning of their favorite television program."

"On Saturday morning?" Yogi Bear, maybe?

"You know, I wondered that, too. Seems they fall asleep before 'Masterpiece Theatre' on Sunday night, but the station runs a repeat at ten-thirty Saturday."

The light dawned. At ten-thirty, he had been taking popovers out of her oven.

"Sit tight," he said. "I'll be right back."

She sat on the spotless sofa listening to the sounds of the house. Murmuring voices, mostly, and heavy feet. An automatic washer spinning. Then Fred and the others calling back and forth.

Torn between fascination and horror, she wished for earlids.

"No prints, Fred. Faucets are wiped clean. He wasn't so careful about the sink, though. Traces of blood here. Probably hers."

"Weapon?" That was Fred. He'd be calm in a hurricane.

"I checked the toilet tank and the laundry hamper. Sheets, towels, kids' clothes. A penny and a couple of nickels. That's it in here."

"No razor?"

"There's an electric shaver. And some Nair."

"Come on back in the bedroom, then. And keep your big feet out of the blood."

Joan shuddered. Although she hadn't seen that gory bedroom, her all too vivid imagination was sparing her nothing.

A dapper little man with a mustache appeared from somewhere behind her, his shining shoes in sharp contrast to the scuffed medical bag he carried. Moments later, two uniformed attendants maneuvered an empty stretcher in the front door and through the living room. The murmuring began again, punctuated by occasional shouts and grunts, and then the stretcher, covered, came back through the bric-a-brac. Joan stood quietly, out of some notion of respect, she supposed, although certainly no one was paying attention to anything she did. She sat down with a feeling of relief. At least the children would be spared that.

Fred returned finally with a slender young man in whose dark features she could see something of George Petris. None of the aggressive impatience she remembered, though. Fred introduced them without mentioning Joan's relationship to the orchestra. Daniel sat stiffly, his hands in his lap.

"I'm sorry you're having such a rough time," Joan said.

He looked as if that was the last thing he'd expected to hear.

"I'm all right."

She plodded on. "It seems to me you've had more than your share of sudden death."

He didn't answer, but began biting a thumbnail.

Fred broke the silence. "Would you mind telling me again what happened?"

"From when?"

"From when you first heard of her."

A smile threatened the corners of Daniel's mouth.

"I was twelve. She was on my paper route."

"How well did you know her?"

"I didn't. She was a customer."

"Good tipper?"

"No, but she never made me wait for the money."

"Do you know her family?"

"I used to see her outside with a baby. Sometimes her husband would be sitting on the porch with a beer when I delivered. We never talked."

"I take it you haven't seen her recently."

"No. I quit the papers after a couple of years."

"Why did you come here this morning?"

"She called me—I think on Thursday—and said she had my father's oboe and I should come for it."

"But you waited until today."

"I was busy. I can't play the thing, anyway."

"Go on."

"So today I called her to see if I could pick it up."

"Did she answer the phone?"

"I guess so." He was suddenly cautious. "I mean, she doesn't have a sister or anything, does she?"

Joan held her breath.

"Relax," Fred said. "I'm not setting traps. Far as I know, she lived here with her husband and three little girls. They're young enough I don't think you could confuse their voices."

"Okay, then, she answered. And she said sure, come on over. So I did. You know what I found." Backing away from the specifics, he gnawed at the corner of a little fingernail.

"What time was that call?"

"I don't know," Daniel said. "Maybe ten, ten-thirty. I didn't want to call early. I mean, it's Saturday, and some people sleep in."

"And you left home right away?"

"Yes."

"That's about a ten-minute drive?"

"I walked. It took maybe half an hour. I don't know." His arms were bare to the elbow. No watch. "It's a couple of miles and I wasn't hurrying."

"Exactly what happened when you got here?"

"I rang the bell, but nobody came. So I rang it again. Still nothing. I figured she couldn't hear the bell. The door was open and I knew she was expecting me, so I called and walked in."

"What made you go into the bedroom?"

"I didn't know it was the bedroom, honest!" A trace of panic had crept into his voice. "I didn't see her here or in the kitchen, so I started down the hall. That was the first door. When I stuck my head in, I saw her lying there in all that blood, just the way you found her."

"Then what?"

"Then I called the cops. I asked for you because you were the only one I knew."

"Think carefully. What did you move?"

"I didn't move anything. I didn't even touch anything. I just backed out and called you."

"On what?"

"Oh...yeah. I touched the phone. That one." He pointed to a little telephone table with a seat, of a sort Joan hadn't seen for at least twenty years. Another doily. "I don't think I moved it any."

"Anything in her room? In the bathroom?"

"I didn't even *go* in those rooms!" The panic was unmistakable now.

"But you felt comfortable walking into her house."

"I'd just talked to her. I told you. She was expecting me."

"To pick up your father's oboe."

"Right."

Very quietly. "Then where's the oboe?"

Daniel's jaw dropped. He sagged back on the sofa. "My God," he said. "I forgot all about it."

Lundquist waited.

"You didn't find it?" Daniel asked. "You aren't putting me on?"

"No, we didn't find it."

Daniel shook his head stupidly and then suddenly came to life. "That proves it!"

"What's that?" Fred asked.

"That I didn't kill her. Oh, I know you suspect me. I didn't have to answer any of these questions, but I know I didn't do it. Don't you see, that proves it. If I killed her, then I'd have the oboe. But I didn't, and I don't."

"Can you think of anyone who might have killed her? Maybe someone who knew your dad, too?"

"Look, I didn't even know they knew each other. She called me up, that's all."

Abruptly, Lundquist stood up.

"Thank you very much."

Daniel looked at him. "That's it?"

"That's it. If you think of anything you'd like to add, you know how to reach me. I'll ask Sergeant Pruitt to take you over to the station to make a formal statement."

He escorted Daniel to the door. Through the window that faced onto the porch, Joan thought she saw a mobile TV unit. Yes, there was the cameraman zeroing in on Daniel. Then Sergeant Pruitt, a bulky man, blocked the camera's view, and they drove off.

She dreaded running that electronic gauntlet when her turn came. She supposed she could leave by the back door—no, then the children would have to come through the house. It might not be so bad, though, if only they didn't have to see their mother's room. Maybe even less frightening than being forbidden to enter their own house entirely.

I hope I can get some of their things for them, she thought. A sudden silence told her that the washer had finished spinning. Maybe she ought to put the laundry in the dryer.

"Well," said Fred beside her, "what did you think?"

"About Daniel? I thought he was used to being suspected of doing something wrong."

He looked at her with the raised eyebrows of respect. She dared a question.

"He sounded genuinely surprised about the oboe, as if he'd forgotten all about it. Is it really missing?"

"We haven't found it. You'd think she'd have it ready, if she knew he was coming. Of course, we haven't found the murder weapon, either, unless it's an ordinary household knife. We're going through every drawer in the house. It's not on Daniel. He asked us to search him and we did."

"And he did call you."

"Well, he couldn't be sure someone hadn't seen him. Discovering the body is an old one. But he did volunteer to answer questions after we read him his rights."

"Not to change the subject, but does everything really have to stay as it is until you solve this?"

"What do you have in mind?"

"Does the family have to get out and leave everything behind? I was thinking that would be awfully hard on them."

"We'll probably seal her room for a few days. I imagine they'll want to be somewhere else until it's cleaned up. We can't do that yet."

"What about clothes and things?"

"They can take what they need. Why?"

"I thought while I'm waiting, maybe I could finish the laundry in case they'll need it. I wouldn't mind."

"What do you mean, finish?"

"I heard the washer shut off when Daniel left. I could put the things in the dryer, if that's okay."

"I'll see if they're done in there yet."

In a few moments he beckoned to her.

"You go right ahead."

After the living room, an orderly kitchen was only to be expected. Something was simmering in a Crock Pot and the dishes in the drainer were covered with a clean towel. An ironing board stood ready, the iron plugged in but not turned on. Dampened rolls in a wicker basket took Joan back to her young married days, before new fabrics—and new attitudes—had changed everything. Well, she'd volunteered; she might as well iron the stuff before it mildewed. Inspecting the contents of the basket briefly, she set the iron on Cotton to heat.

When she opened the lid of the washer, she thought for a moment it was empty. Centrifugal force had flattened the two bulky items against the tub's perforations, embossing little round bumps on their terry cloth surfaces, which she saw when she peeled them off the sides and tossed them into the dryer.

A sudden thought stopped her hand before it touched the knob.

"Fred," she called.

He came with that rapid but unhurried walk she'd seen earlier.

"Look at these. They're wet."

"You expected dry?"

"Fred, I'm serious."

"You'd better tell me." A certain I'm-being-patient-with-this-nonsense tone.

"Fred, this tells us she was still alive about forty minutes ago."

The respect was missing from his raised eyebrows this time.

"Sure," she insisted. "I used to have almost the twin of this machine. Set like this, it takes about forty minutes from start to finish. I heard it when I came in and I told you just now when it went off. Maybe Daniel heard it, too, without hearing it, if you know what I mean. Remember, he said he thought she couldn't hear the doorbell?"

Now he was nodding. He reached into the dryer and shook out a large white bath towel and a blue terrycloth robe with a hood.

"Forty minutes, you say?"

"Mine would take that long. A little less, maybe, if she set it to wash six minutes instead of twelve. You can't tell that. Most of it is the filling and spinning time, though. This one is set on regular, extra high, with a cold wash and cold rinse—the things are cold, aren't they? That usually takes longer than a warm rinse, because water comes in from only one faucet. It's easy enough to check. Just start it. It won't matter whether there's anything in it or not."

"We'll do that. I think, on the whole, you'd better not dry these. I'll keep them. We might need a statement from you about hearing the washer."

He bore the wet things off. Joan sighed. She hitched up her jeans and wiped her forehead. Testing the iron's sizzle with two wet fingers, she unwrapped the first blue cotton bundle and set herself to a chore she hadn't faced at home in months.

Ironing wasn't her idea of fun, but it beat sitting in that painfully neat parlor doing nothing while the police carried out their routine. She welcomed the physical task that left her mind free even as she resented the man who would expect his wife to iron cotton work shirts. No, that wasn't fair. Wanda probably chose them herself. They went with the doilies.

♩♩♩

By the time the uniformed officer came to tell her that Mr. Borowski had come home, she knew something didn't make sense. Thinking about it was like trying to get a good look at one of the little floaters in her eye. When she'd aim at it, it would slide off in the opposite direction, only to swim back annoyingly into her peripheral vision where she couldn't focus clearly.

# Chapter Thirteen

Stanislaus Borowski kept repeating himself.

He stood in the middle of the living room, his arms outstretched and his calloused hands squeezing the air in front of him. Sweat stained his familiar blue cotton shirt.

"She was fine when I left home," he was saying. "How's a guy supposed to know a thing like this is gonna happen? They call me for some overtime. She's fine, the kids are fine, I go. A man's gotta work, you know? Why'd anybody do a thing like this? How'm I supposed to know? My God, they didn't even take the cash off the dresser. Why'd anybody want to do a thing like this?"

"We all want to know, Mr. Borowski," Lundquist said. "We want to get the person who did it."

"How's that gonna help me, huh? Where's that leave me? How's that gonna take care of the kids? My God, she was fine this morning."

From the kitchen doorway, Joan recognized his outraged disbelief and overtones of guilt. Clothed in pious words, or expressed as openly as this, it was a part of grief she knew all too well. She had reacted to Ken's death with stunned silence and tears, but the monologue inside her head would have shocked many of her friends.

She waited for a cue from Fred. It came.

"Mr. Borowski, this is Mrs. Spencer. She knew your wife and is willing to take the children home with her today, while you get your bearings. Would that help?"

He seemed to notice her for the first time. He dropped his hands.

"Thanks, lady, but no, thanks. I'll call my sister." He wheeled around to face Fred. "Where are they, anyhow?"

"Your neighbors say they went to the park a couple of hours ago. We have a man looking."

"I gotta find 'em. You do anything you want to about that damn killer. I gotta find my girls." He charged out the front door, ignoring the crowd.

Fred motioned to a plainclothesman. "Stick with him, Joe, and phone in when you know the kids are safe. We'll talk to him later."

Churning inside, Joan found her purse and left.

♩♩♩

Hours later, Lundquist unlocked his own door. The smell hit him first, and the phone started ringing before he made it to the kitchen. He knew what was coming, but it was worse than he had imagined. Both ways.

Tucking the receiver between a shoulder and an ear, he began scraping dough off the tabletop and floor. "Hello."

"Fred, where on earth have you been?" Catherine's voice combined whining and demanding into one shrill tone. "Do you have any idea what time it is?"

"Pushing seven?" He peeled the once-wet towels off the stickiness overflowing his two-foot wooden proofing bowls and resisted the temptation to throw the scrapings back in. Sure, the bread would be sterile after an hour in a hot oven, but no one would tolerate finding even a sterile hair in a sandwich.

"I came by to pick up the bread two hours ago and I've called every fifteen minutes since. What do you think you're doing?"

"Well, Catherine, I'll tell you. I think I'm doing my job. We had a little emergency today."

"I'm coming now."

"No, wait." He caught her before she hung up. "Don't. I didn't bake it."

"You what?" Her dismay deafened him.

"I didn't even get it into the pans. I'm sorry. I should have warned you sooner."

Risen and then fallen back on itself, the bread would be dry at best. Edible, maybe, if he skipped the second rising and baked the loaves immediately after shaping them.

Her voice yammered on as if one batch of sourdough were the be-all and end-all. He half-listened while punching down what hadn't landed on the floor. The dough didn't fight back. It lay in the bowls inertly, without elasticity. There was no point in letting her go on.

"Catherine, I really am sorry. There's nothing I can do with this stuff. The best I can offer is to stop by Brackett's for you. Their cottage cheese dill bread is good, and their pumpernickel."

"Forget it. I'll manage."

He pulled the receiver away from his ear just in time. Even at arm's length he could hear her slam down the phone. He suspected her of smashing it onto a table before hanging up. It wasn't the first time. The next step in the dance, he knew, was for him to arrive on her doorstep with flowers and apologies. Poised to rush off to her party, she would accept with a devastating graciousness that stung worse than the anger she was dishing out now. Not tonight. He wasn't up to being devastated.

He dumped the dough into the wet garbage. Let Milligan's pigs party tomorrow.

When the phone rang again, he didn't bother to hide his fatigue. "Yeah?"

"Fred, it's Joan. Am I interrupting your supper?"

"No, I just walked in. Problem?" He leaned against the wall, afraid to sit down.

"I'm all right. I've been thinking about Wanda and I may have figured out a connection. Would you like to come over? We haven't eaten yet either. There's plenty."

"I'm on my way."

♭♭♭

She fed him first. One look at his face had told her that much. Andrew, too, seemed to recognize Fred's weariness. He kept up a line of patter that required little response, avoiding what was on all their minds.

Over coffee in the living room, Joan finally brought it up.

"Did they find the children, Fred?"

"Oh, sure. They were on their way home. Borowski broke it to them and took them to their aunt's. They're pretty tough."

"He was taking it hard. You don't suspect him, do you?"

"We did, of course. There was no break-in. No sign of an intruder. Nothing was stolen, not even her grandmother's silver from Poland. She wasn't beaten or raped. She probably let the killer in. The door was open and the screen was unhooked."

Joan thought with a sinking feeling of her own wide-open house. Fred went on.

"The neighbors say she was careful, but she seems to have trusted the killer enough to walk into the bedroom while he was there. There's no sign of force. Sure, we suspected him. According to the neighbors, their home life wasn't all that peaceful. Actually, they said she did most of the yelling. If he'd been killed, I'd have to be looking at her."

"I wondered if she was hard to live with. I was thinking more of the kids, though."

"It doesn't matter. Stan Borowski spent the morning fixing a broken water main across from the post office. He was on a six-man crew from seven-thirty until we found him. He's clear, short of putting out a contract on his wife, and that I don't see."

"No. Fred, the oboe is the obvious connection, isn't it?"

"Which we don't have."

"Which the murderer probably took. Even if it was Daniel. When Andrew carried the paper, he knew every shortcut and garbage can on his route. Daniel could have hidden the oboe somewhere. The case isn't all that big. If Wanda called him as he said she did, he'd have to come back. For all he'd know, she might have told someone else he was coming, and then not showing up would be something he'd have to explain away."

"And the weapon might be with the oboe," he said. "Could be."

"It might have been with it all along."

"Come again?"

"Fred, have you ever seen a reed knife?"

"A reed knife?"

"It looks a little bit like a straight razor, but it doesn't fold up. At least the ones I've seen don't. You know, those double reeds on oboes and bassoons cost a small fortune, and they're so unreliable that most players cut their own. It's the only way to get them the way they want them. They almost all shape them, even if they buy them ready-made. A real snob like George wouldn't dream of that, though."

"I never got past a number two Rico sax reed in the marching band."

"Sax and clarinet reeds are cheaper. Not so many people bother. But good players work them over, too, and when they get one they like, they save it for performances."

"You think Petris had a reed knife with his oboe?"

"I know he had one. I saw him using it."

"And this knife would be strong enough—you didn't see her, did you?"

"They look plenty strong to me. You could check Sam's or Elmer's."

"Is the whole orchestra armed to the teeth?"

"Hardly. The other bassoonist probably has one. The clarinets might. Why would they want to kill Wanda?"

"Why would anyone? This isn't narrowing it down. If the knife was in the oboe case and she had it out for Daniel, anyone could have used it. For that matter, a sharp pocket-knife could probably have done the job."

"I keep coming back to that oboe," she said. "Maybe somebody wanted it. Maybe that's why they were both killed."

"Who would want an oboe?"

"I don't know, but it's gone. Of course, it might not have been the oboe at all. The murderer could have taken it so we wouldn't notice that the knife was missing. Maybe George was killed for some other reason and Wanda was too close to him. If she saw something important and remembered it, that would make her too dangerous. Maybe she was just in the wrong place at the wrong time."

"Can you draw me a map? Where was everybody when Petris collapsed?"

She tried. It was all out of proportion, but it did place the violins on the conductor's left, with the firsts on the outside and the seconds next to them. On the far right, she put the cellos and beside them, the violas. In the inner circle of the fan-shaped orchestra, she drew the first stand of each of the strings, except, of course, the basses, who stood at the back. In the second row were two cellos, John Hocking, Joan, Sam Wade, George Petris,

Wanda Borowski, another flute, and four violins. Behind herself, Joan remembered a space not quite big enough to protect her ears from the trumpets. Behind Sam sat the demoted lady bassoonist; behind George, Elmer Rush; and to his right, the clarinets. Across the back row were the basses, the tuba, Nancy and the other trombones, the horns, and, on the far side, the tympani.

Fred led her again through the story of George's collapse and the end of the rehearsal. Nothing new.

"Do you remember where any of these people were when the refreshments were being served?"

"I've gone over it a dozen times in my mind. About all I can tell you are some who didn't have any."

"That might be a start."

"John didn't leave his seat. He's dieting. His daughter was doing homework. The horns were practicing and so was one of the trumpets. I could find out which one, but I'd guess it was the first. Sam stayed put, too, thank goodness. I would have been the first casualty if he hadn't been there to catch me when I tripped on my own big feet. A lot of people went outside to beat the heat, but I don't know how many of them stopped at the table. The concertmaster was out, I know. He took his sweet time coming back. Not much help, is it?"

"Was Petris one of the ones who went out?"

"I don't know. Not for long, if he did. He did have a drink. I think Nancy said Glenda Wallston served him."

"Oh, she did, did she?"

"You've heard that story?"

"Not from you," he said.

"I told you there was gossip."

"There sure is," Andrew said. "I heard about Lisa Wallston from Jennifer."

"I'll look into it." Fred didn't tell them what Daniel had already confirmed.

"Fred, I don't believe half the things I've heard about George," Joan said. "You'd think death would make people kinder, but it seems to do just the opposite." She tried to sip from her empty coffee cup and put it down absently. "It's obscene to go digging into his life like that."

"This isn't just death, Joan. This is murder. If you're right, then those three children are motherless because someone wanted to kill George Petris. We don't know who that someone is or what he might do next, or why. It doesn't even matter what was true about Petris. What matters is what someone out there believes. What would be obscene would be to hold back anything now that might help prevent still another murder."

"You don't think…" Her voice trailed off.

"I do think. I think you're right about why Wanda Borowski was killed. I spent the afternoon talking with people about her. Family, friends, neighbors, even her priest. Nothing. If there's no connection to Petris, I'm lost, and the only one I can see besides Daniel and the oboe itself is the orchestra. I think any one of you could be in danger, especially the people who sat near enough to Petris to see whatever she might have seen."

He consulted her drawing. "I'll warn Sam. He's the next closest. And those two bassoon players behind them. Don't take any chances yourself, Joan. I can't tell you to watch out for strangers. It's probably not a stranger. Just—don't trust anyone too far, you hear?"

Andrew cleared his throat noisily.

"In that case, I better tell you," he said. "You remember, Mom, Jennifer was afraid she'd never get into music school if Mr. Petris judged the concerto competition this year."

"Mmm."

"While I was working in the lab, Mr. Werner said Jennifer went out with Daniel Petris for an egg roll. I nearly choked when I heard that. And then later one of the other professors came in and started talking about how Petris screwed up the biology requirements when he was dean. You could tell Mr. Werner didn't want to talk about it, but the other guy wouldn't shut up. He said he'd thought they were safe with Werner on the curriculum committee to stand up to Petris, but then Petris made monkeys out of all of them. Mr. Werner didn't like that. He's pretty quiet, but he got all red in the face and said he fought the S.O.B.— that's what he called him—he fought him every way he could, but you couldn't win against a dean like that. If Jennifer knew how he felt, maybe she helped Daniel get the poison."

There went the fingers through his hair again, just like his father's. Suddenly it was hitting too close.

"Andrew, I don't think you should go back there."

"To the lab? Come on, Mom, you don't mean that. I'm maybe right in the middle of a murder and you want me to leave now and miss everything? I notice you took off like an ambulance chaser when you got that phone call today. Why should you have all the fun?"

"Andrew!"

"Admit it, Mom. You left this big mess—which, by the way, *I* picked up—just so you could play detective."

She bristled.

"I wasn't playing anything. I even did the ironing over there." He knew how she felt about ironing.

"There. Not here."

Joan sat speechless. Serpents' teeth couldn't spread butter compared to this child, she thought. Pay the bills, do the laundry, that's me.

"Everyone thinks you're so good to people," Andrew continued relentlessly. "They don't know you're just nosy. Why you expect me to be any different?"

That last sentence and the grin that went with it cut through the guilt she'd been hearing him pile on her. Suddenly she saw the funny side of it all. He had her dead to rights, but it no longer threatened her. She turned to Lundquist, her eyes dancing.

"What do you think, Fred? Is a mouth like that safe out in public?"

"He does all right," Fred said, dodging the squabble. "If you're asking whether it's safe to go back to the lab, I don't know why not. In fact, I could use an insider. What you told us tonight may turn out to be important, Andrew. But don't confide in anyone but me. The less you talk, the safer you'll be. Listen all you like, but stay away from keyholes. Leave the fancy stuff to the professionals."

Andrew nodded soberly.

"And, Joan, if you remember anything more about the night Petris died, don't put off letting me know. You may know something you don't realize is important and it could be worth your life."

They were both quiet after he left. Andrew cleared the table without being asked and spread out his pre-calculus. Standing at the kitchen sink, Joan saw her own face reflected in the dark glass.

The window was a perfect one-way mirror at night; anyone going by would be able to see her clearly.

For the first time since moving back to Oliver, she snapped the shutters tight.

# Chapter Fourteen

The Sunday *Courier* screamed bloody murder. A fuzzy snapshot of Wanda Borowski and her children smiled beside a photograph of the crowd gawking at that covered stretcher and the natty little man identified as Dr. James Henshaw, county coroner.

Most of the information on the case was attributed to "Lieutenant Fred Lundquist, veteran of the Oliver police force and formerly high point man on the special Indianapolis detective squad that solved the so-called Hoosier Hysteria murders that marred little Clear Creek's one and only championship in the Indiana High School Athletic Association basketball tourney."

Lundquist groaned. Bob Peterson never had made the mental switch from the sports page to page one. It might have been worse, though. There were no glaring inaccuracies.

"According to Dr. Henshaw, Wanda Borowski died within moments of the fatal blow," he read. "Neither the weapon nor a suicide note was found. Borowski, 5–2 and 105 pounds, showed no signs of having resisted her attacker. Discovered lying in a pool of congealing blood on the bedroom floor, her body was fully clothed. She had not been abused sexually."

The paper told no more than he wanted revealed at this point. Bob had kept his promise not to get in the way. Enterprising as usual, he had noticed that this was the symphony's second sudden death in a week. Without knowing who had discovered the body, he had proposed a feature about orchestral murders, maybe with a Phantom of the Opera angle.

Fred had been plain: "I can't stop you. Go ahead, print the name of every last fiddler. Drag in the tuba and the tympani. Hamstring the investigation. Those people can't help but be alert when I come around, but they might think of Sam Wade as just another player if you don't screw things up. Think your cute story is worth it?"

Apparently not. Mention of the orchestra was buried in the tame little obituary on page two, surrounded by Wanda's church and volunteer activities. Bob had made the most of the children's fresh-scrubbed innocence, their father's grief, and their mother's quiet lifestyle and spotless housekeeping. He featured the shocked reaction of the two old neighbor ladies who worried about what the world was coming to "if a woman can have her throat slashed in her own home in broad daylight for no good reason."

Fred wondered what reason they would consider sufficient.

Licking a last crumb of doughnut glaze from his fingers, he folded the paper napkin he used for a breakfast plate, rinsed out his coffee mug, and checked his watch. At ten o'clock he shouldn't rouse too many people out of bed, even on a Sunday. He consulted the personnel list Nakamura had given him and started on his rounds.

Elmer Rush was already out.

"I'm sorry. Was he expecting you?" The slender woman with freckles and faded red hair already looked tired. A dustcloth hung from her pocket.

"I took a chance. Do you expect him back soon?"

"I couldn't say. What are you selling?"

When he identified himself, some of the lines in her face relaxed.

"Come in, won't you? I really expect him back any time, but I don't like to say much to just anybody. I'm Martha Lambert, his daughter. He's not himself today and I didn't want him bothered by another door-to-door salesman. We seem to get a steady stream of them."

She led him into a room furnished mostly with well-polished antiques of the simplest, straightest lines. Rag rugs warmed the old floor and plain muslin curtains gave the windows a clean, fresh look. The sofa, on the other hand, had been through the wars. She followed his glance and smiled ruefully.

"I've given up worrying, what with three kids and a dog. Besides, who has money these days for furniture? Tell me, officer, what do you want with my dad?" Her face changed suddenly and she clutched the dustcloth as if for support. "Has something happened?"

"No, it's just routine. I understand he plays in the Oliver Civic Symphony."

"That's right."

"I'm checking facts in a couple of cases involving members of the orchestra. I'm sorry if he's ill."

"He's all right. Sit down, please."

Avoiding the dog hair, he chose a Shaker chair. She paced, absently pulling the cloth through her fingers.

"He's not sick, but it's a bad day. He gets these fierce moods sometimes when he'd not fit to live with. I was glad he decided to take a walk. He took Julie in her chair so he could really move along. It'll do them both good, I hope." She crossed the room.

"Julie's your daughter?" She nodded. "I saw them together the other day at the Senior Citizens' Center," he said.

"I didn't realize you'd met."

"We haven't. I was talking to someone who works there and his name was mentioned. He seems devoted to Julie."

"He's been trying to make it up to us, ever since it happened."

"Pardon me?"

"Julie almost drowned once because of a couple of kids we trusted her with cared more about cheap thrills than about her. Dad came along in time to save her life—he about killed the lifeguard—but she's been retarded ever since. It was easier when my husband was alive, but I swear, I think it shortened his life. Now I don't know what I'd do without Dad. Only sometimes..." She crossed the room again, and stared out the window.

"Sometimes?"

"Sometimes he scares me. He scared me a lot when I was little. Then when I left home, I forgot, and when I saw him on visits he was generally on his good behavior. Now...now it's the way I remember it. He's all sweetness and love one minute, and the next, you think he'll slap you down if you look at him crooked. I've seen him go into rages at strangers. When I was in school my friends wouldn't spend the night with me. I know my mother never crossed him." Her voice shrank. "I leave him with Julie so much. What if he hurts her?"

Lundquist pulled out a card and wrote swiftly on the back.

"This is the crisis number of the women's shelter nearest us. It's answered day and night. And I'll respond if you call me. Has he ever touched you?"

"Hit me? No." Very small now. "He spanked me sometimes when I was a little girl."

"Julie?"

"I don't think so, but how could I be sure she'd tell me?" The tears spilled. She brushed at them, smudging her cheeks.

"I think you'd guess," he said. "Does she act afraid of him? Have you ever seen bruises or scrapes, or even a red spot?"

"No."

He unfolded a clean handkerchief and held it out. She wiped her eyes and blew her nose loudly.

"Thank you," she said. "You've helped me a lot."

His big hand patted her shoulder clumsily. I'm no good at this sort of thing, he thought.

"I'll be back," he said. "I really do want to ask your father a couple of questions."

"You won't say anything to him?"

"Don't worry."

She was still standing in the doorway when he drove away. He glimpsed his own white handkerchief, waving.

♮♮♮

Joan, too, began Sunday morning with the *Courier*. She learned nothing from Peterson's story. For once, she knew more than the paper. Turning to Wanda's obituary, she read that funeral arrangements were still pending. She wondered how long it took for the police to collect all the evidence a body could give them.

Another name leaped at her from the obituaries: Walter Bergdorfer. She remembered at once the irascible old man who had shouted at her and all the other neighborhood children for hopping the chain he'd strung across his lawn to discourage them from beating a path in the grass as they cut the corner. She had never felt guilt, but only mild triumph at clearing the hurdle.

The paper gave Mr. Bergdorfer's age as seventy-three. Joan realized with a start that she was now within spitting distance of being as old as the decrepit grouch she remembered had been.

The phone interrupted her count of her gray hairs. At the sound of Nancy's voice, Joan girded herself for a long session of "Isn't it awful?" and was relieved when Nancy paid mere lip service to the murder and invited her instead to represent the orchestra at the hospital. Charlotte Hodden, the little cellist, had produced a baby boy on Saturday.

"Didn't you see it in the birth announcements? Someone ought to go. She's a sweet little thing, very faithful. I bet she's back at rehearsal within two weeks."

"Nancy, I'm glad you noticed. I didn't even know her name yet. Do you want to take flowers?"

"That's why I called you. The orchestra usually buys them, but you know Yoichi isn't going to brave an OB ward. Actually, Evelyn suggested you. She wants to go, but she says she's too busy to pick up flowers. Didn't I tell you?"

Joan refrained from pointing out that Nancy herself might know her way to a florist.

"All right. How much do I spend?" I may as well check prices on funeral bouquets while I'm at it, she thought.

"I think around ten—ask Yoichi. The Rose Basket's good and they donate to the orchestra. Just don't let them fob blue carnations off on you. I can't stand them."

"Trust me." Or do it yourself. "When are visiting hours?"

They settled on two o'clock.

Yoichi welcomed her call. "I am a little stiff and sore today," he said. "I fell off my bicycle yesterday."

"No broken bones, I hope."

"No, only some scratches. Do you know how to get blood out of a white sweater? I am afraid I have ruined the one my mother gave me when I went home to Japan this summer. She made it herself."

"Cold water. Let it soak a long time. Then wash it the way you usually do. Bleach helps, but you mustn't use it on wool."

She had answered automatically, but her thoughts raced ahead after she hung up. Yoichi worried about bloodstained clothing the day after Wanda's throat was cut? Yoichi? He had been on the scene when George died, in a good position to be sure that no one revived him in time. But why would he have told her about the poison at all? Surely it would have been safer to let everyone go on believing in a sudden illness.

Joan poured herself another cup of coffee and tried to read the rest of the paper. Her mind refused to follow the words on the page.

Maybe Yoichi had planned to say nothing. Then Wanda had seen something and the emergency room doctor had turned out to be Japanese, a man who might have guessed the truth about Japanese puffer fish poison on his own. Far better to blow the whistle and sound innocent.

But why Yoichi?

Why anybody? Fred's question came back to her. It wasn't hard to imagine that anyone might hate George Petris, but she found it impossible to think that the soft-spoken young man she knew would commit cold-blooded murder. And not once, but twice.

Don't be silly, she told herself. If he did it, you don't know him at all. All you know is the act he's been putting on for your benefit. It would explain why he unburdened himself to you when he'd scarcely met you. And you thought it was your good listening ear. He's certainly thorough, if he even scratched himself to explain away any blood he picked up.

Feeling foolish but sure that he wouldn't laugh, she called Fred to relay her latest brainstorm. No answer. She'd try again after the hospital.

# Chapter Fifteen

With the glowing, slightly overstuffed look of new mothers everywhere, Charlotte Hodden seemed a little flustered by her visitors. Small wonder, Joan thought. Evelyn Wade was playing gracious lady to the hilt. (Joan had felt Nancy's nudge when Evelyn had deftly relieved her of the chrysanthemums on their way down the long hospital corridor.)

She herself was inclined to the opinion that half the reason for having a baby in the hospital was to escape all social obligations for at least a few days. Now, fifteen minutes after their arrival, she was sure they had become such an obligation. She tried a couple of graceful exit lines, but neither Nancy (who, indeed, might not know better) or Evelyn (who should) showed signs of budging from the two comfortable guest chairs in the semi-private room. Joan was sitting on the edge of the second bed, which was temporarily empty. She stood up and made another attempt.

"Is there anything we could do for you while you're getting your strength back?" Maybe that would remind them.

"Oh, I couldn't ask you…"

"Anything, dear," Evelyn gushed. "I remember how long it took me after ours were born. Of course, it's even harder with the second—there's never a moment to rest—though the delivery itself isn't so bad."

"What do you need?" Joan asked, hoping to nip any more maternal reminiscing in the bud.

"It's my cello."

That stopped them.

"You don't expect to practice here!" Evelyn sounded shocked. Not unless obstetrics has taken a giant leap, Joan thought, wincing as she pictured the edge-of-the-chair posture favored by many cellists.

Charlotte giggled. "Wouldn't that set them on their ears?"

"What, then?" Nancy asked.

"Well, you know, the baby wasn't really due for another week or two. He kind of took me by surprise. And my cello needs some work. I had it all fixed with Mr. Isaac that I'd take it to him next week, so it would be ready by the time I could start playing again. I suppose I could have left it with him on the way over here Friday, but that was the last thing on our minds, especially Ed's. It was all I could do to convince him I wouldn't drop the baby in the shower. Anyhow, the cello's at home and I just know Ed's not going to want to mess with it."

Joan expected Evelyn to deliver them from the pregnant silence that followed, but an unruly mum suddenly needed to be coaxed into a more artistic place. Oh, well.

"I haven't found Isaac's shop yet," she said. "Where is it?"

"Just across the street from the old depot—only that's a tavern now," Nancy answered. "Of course, I never go to him. He's strictly strings. You'd be the natural, Joan."

Mmm. "I do need a couple of strings. How can I pick up the cello?"

"You're sure? Please don't go to a lot of trouble on my account," Charlotte said, looking relieved.

"I'm sure."

"Ed's home today, probably watching the ball game. I'll warn him to expect you to call." She beamed. "This is such a help. Thank you a lot. Mr. Isaac is going to work on the fingerboard and cut me a new bridge so I can play above third position on the inside strings. I just hope I can still manage lessons, what with the baby and all. I didn't expect to be so tired."

"I don't wonder you're tired," said a voice behind Joan. A nurse had entered the room on soundless soles, without the warning starched skirts once gave. Her brisk cheerfulness belied the dark circles under her own eyes. She pulled the hermetically sealed venetian blinds to darken the room slightly.

"You didn't get much sleep in thirty hours of labor," she said. "I can guarantee you won't get much after you go home, either. You've had a big visit now. Try to rest some before the babies are out again."

"Glenda! How nice to see you here," said Evelyn, turning from the flowers.

"Hello, Evelyn. Don't look so surprised; I work here, you know. And it really is time to leave."

"Oh, Glenda, please show them the baby!" Charlotte begged. "I almost feel as if he was yours, the way you stuck with me. She was so great," she said to the women now being herded out the door.

"I will."

Glenda kept her promise, stopping at the nursery window to point out a baby with a minuscule chin and a mop of black hair.

"Did you really stay with her thirty hours?" Nancy asked.

"No, of course not. I only work from seven to three. But I was here when she first came in, and then things were so quiet yesterday that I could almost special her. She was alone and scared. That Ed Hodden is no prize. He dropped her here and went off to do his worrying in a bar, from the looks of him when he finally showed up. We talked a lot until her labor picked up. She's a sweet girl."

A quick look at her name tag confirmed Joan's suspicion that this was Glenda Wallston, the symphony guild member whose daughter had been entangled with the Petris men. It was easy to understand her lack of sympathy for the sins of the fathers.

"I'm glad the orchestra sent flowers," Glenda went on. "Ed sure didn't. Are we doing something about Wanda, too?"

"I've checked with the undertaker," Joan said. "When the plans are settled, we'll do whatever is appropriate. We don't have the word on a memorial for George Petris yet, either, but I assume we will." Nor had anyone brought up the question. It seemed as good a time as any.

Glenda didn't turn a hair. "I suppose. Should I know you?"

Nancy introduced them. "Glenda's a member of the symphony guild, Joan. But of course, you saw her at rehearsal. She and Evelyn did the refreshments last Wednesday, remember?"

For once, Joan did remember. "That's right. You told me she served George. We've all been trying to remember, Glenda. Did

George drink anything, or did he just eat cookies? I'm sure you've heard there's some question about his death."

"I wouldn't know. I was filling cups and Evelyn was handing them out. A lot of people just picked them up. I doubt if he ate anything, though."

"That's right," Evelyn said. "Sam always waits until after he's played. Most of the wind players do. We usually keep something out for them."

"Did you give him a cup, Evelyn?" Nancy asked.

"I don't remember. All that fuss, now really. I'm sure the man died of a heart attack, the way the doctor said. Your punch isn't that bad, Glenda."

No one laughed. Glenda looked pointedly at her watch.

"Sorry I can't stay to chat, but some of us have to make a living."

She stepped behind the nurse's desk and flipped open a chart.

Evelyn sailed out of the ward with her chin high. Joan and Nancy trailed in her wake.

"I don't see what got her so hot and bothered," Evelyn said as they stood waiting for the elevators, which seemed to be running in convoys.

"Is there a Mr. Wallston?" Joan asked.

"Not around here," Nancy answered. "He flew the coop years ago. Left Glenda with nothing—no money, no house, no car, no job. Just Lisa, who was about five. Fortunately, Glenda finished her training before she met the bum. She's managed, but it hasn't been any picnic."

"Did I say it had?" Evelyn asked huffily.

No, of course not, Joan thought. All you did was loll around in your Ultrasuede suit and your alligator shoes, looking as if you'd never washed a dish, much less a bed-pan. Then you cracked jokes about her punch. You're lucky she didn't punch you.

Aloud, she said, "I think she was just tired. I know the feeling."

Nancy dropped Evelyn off first.

"Can you believe her?" she asked. "I know I have it easy compared to Glenda, but I don't think Evelyn has the faintest idea of what work is all about. You'd never catch her doing what you did over at Wanda's."

Joan's head swiveled in astonishment.

"Oh, I heard about that," Nancy said. "Things get around in Oliver. Actually, one of the fingerprint guys lives down the street from us. He didn't think his wife would have gone over there in the first place, much less done the laundry. And I can tell you for a fact that Evelyn wouldn't stoop to such a thing. I don't think she could iron a shirt if she had to. I'll bet it's been years since she even changed a bed."

"She did look elegant today."

"I would, too, if I spent the time and money she does shopping and at the beauty parlor. She was complaining that it took her all day yesterday to find those shoes. I didn't think there were that many shoes to choose from in Oliver. She shopped all morning on foot and then went back in the afternoon to try on everything over again. I feel for the clerks."

"At least she bought some."

"True. I'd hate to keep her in clothes, but I suppose it does help the local economy. Wonder if Sam makes her shop in town."

"Very politic of him."

Nancy looked blank for the briefest of moments. "He's a good politician, all right. But that Evelyn."

"Mmm." Saved by the driveway. "Thanks for the ride, Nancy. I'll see you Wednesday. I hope to goodness I find some time between now and then to practice. This has been a wicked week." In more ways than one.

"Don't forget the cello!" Nancy called, and was gone.

# Chapter Sixteen

Checking the phone book, Joan found that Isaac's Violin Studio kept a Saturday rather than a Sunday sabbath. Might as well get it over with.

Ed Hodden answered the doorbell barefoot and barechested, a can of beer in one hand and the cello dangling precariously from the other by the frayed strap of its canvas case. Joan hugged it to her side like a drunken friend and was glad she had when the strap broke while she was wrestling with the door to the studio.

Squeezed between a pizza parlor and a pawnshop, the violin shop was distinctly grubby, at least on the outside. Joan looked across the street at the depot-turned-tavern and remembered vaguely going there with her father to meet someone's train.

It seemed like a strange neighborhood for a music shop. Maybe the rent was low. She found it hard to imagine that Oliver could support someone who dealt only in strings, unless he included guitars.

A little bell jingled as she pulled the stubborn door shut. No clerk stood behind the small counter, but a voice called out, "Be right with you." Joan held the cello carefully by the neck, resting it on its endpin. Violins of all sizes hung from nails on the walls around her, supported by miniature nooses. With a body no more than six or seven inches long, the smallest looked like one of the plastic toy fiddles once sold in dime stores. It might be an eighth size or maybe even a sixteenth. What kind of tone could such a tiny box possibly produce?

She was fascinated by a full-sized violin missing most of its top and back. It looked like bare bones. At first she thought it must be in for repair, but then she could see that it was beautifully finished as it was. Fully strung, it even had a chin rest.

"Whatever for?" she wondered aloud.

"For your world tour. Very useful for practicing in hotel rooms. No one complains when you play out your jet lag at three in the morning. No one else hears."

Short, bent, and with the remains of a crop of wiry curls fringing his ears with gray, the man coming through the door from the back of the shop had to be Mr. Isaac.

"Do you sell a lot of those?" Joan asked.

"Not too many people around here make world tours," he admitted. "On the other hand, once they start thinking about the possibilities, quite a few take a look at a good heavy practice mute. It really cuts down the sound. Wouldn't you like one for your cello? Very reasonable, and when the children are sleeping you can practice in peace, without waking them."

"You flatter me," she said. "It's years since I had a child who went to bed before I did. Besides, this is Charlotte Hodden's cello, not mine. She's the one who's going to need a practice mute."

"I remember. I'm going to raise the fingerboard to two and a half inches and cut a bridge with some curve to it while she's having a baby. I don't know how she could play, as flat as it is now."

"That's it, but the baby didn't wait for you, so she asked me to bring the cello over." She handed it to him, pointing out the broken strap.

"Boy or girl?" he asked, reaching around the cello's curve for a handhold.

"A boy. Lots of hair."

"And how is she doing?"

"Fine. She's tired."

"You tell her not to worry. The cello will be ready before she is."

"I'll tell her. And I need some strings myself."

"Let me put this in a safe place first. What strings do you want?"

"A viola A and G."

"Come on back in the shop. Watch your feet."

She followed him into a room crowded with cases and larger instruments. Several cellos and a bass lay on their sides. Violins and violas in varying states of repair hung from their scrolls in a rack that was a cross between a shadow box and the pipe rack Andrew had once proudly presented his non-smoking father. Compartments under the stripped-down violins held pegs, end buttons, chin rests, bridges, tail pieces, snarls of strings, tuners, and other less easily identifiable bits, presumably to keep them together while the instruments were in the shop. Three shoulder rests under the same violin made Joan wonder how well the system worked.

Bows in need of rehairing hung from nails on another wall, some from the frog and others from the tip, each labeled with a little white sticker on the frog. Hanks of horsehair, both white and black, dangled above one workbench, and blank bridges of all sizes were threaded like fish on a stringer over another. A mended violin top lay on the first bench, cushioned by a scrap of carpet. Half a dozen clamps held its newly glued bass bar in place, and square wooden cleats reinforced a long crack.

Joan recognized vises, clamps, and files. She wasn't so sure about some awl-shaped tools in several sizes. In an odd assortment of small jars and bottles, mostly baby food jars, she could see fluids, from clear to amber to dark brown. Varnish, she supposed. Maybe glue? A familiar white bottle of Elmer's lay on its side in the clutter, but she knew violins predated Elmer's. Dust motes danced in the sunshine above the workbenches.

"Would you mind taking the case with you?" Isaac asked. "I'm very short of space."

"Yes, I can see that."

He unzipped the canvas, tagged the cello, and gave her the case and a receipt for the instrument.

"Don't bend that case too far—the bow's still in there. Now, tell me, what kind of strings did you have in mind?"

"I could really use some advice," she said. "I want a good sound, mostly for orchestral playing, but I can't afford Eudoxas now and my viola chews up gut A strings, even if they're wrapped."

"It shouldn't do that. Bring it in. Maybe there's a rough spot I could file down. In the meantime, why don't you try a Jargar A? It's chrome steel on steel, and I think the tone is better than the Eudoxa steel A. For the G, you could move down to the domestic

Gold Label. That's still silver on gut, but you'll save more than three dollars on a single string."

She took his suggestions gratefully and watched him sort out her new G string from the bunches of little identifying tags sticking out of the transparent storage tubes on the wall like so many long-stemmed flowers. He presented it for her inspection and gave her a flexible plastic tube to protect it. The Jargar A came coiled in a white envelope—not such a good sign, but she'd try it.

"You know," she said, as he wrote up the sale, "I'm really surprised to find you here."

"Why is that?"

"Oliver is such a small town. I can't help wondering how you stay in business."

"I keep busy enough," he said. "It's true that I'd go under if I had to depend on Oliver alone. We have customers all over the country through our catalog."

"I wouldn't have thought there were this many instruments to repair here. Do you do that by mail, too?"

"A lot of them do come from out of town. We contract with a dozen school systems to do all their string repair work. Those kids are hard on school instruments. The teachers do a lot of the little routine jobs, but they can't handle a crack like the one over there." He gestured to the mended violin top Joan had noticed earlier.

"And sometimes I sell one of my own instruments," he said. "I'm almost finished with a viola now. People know I'm here. I don't need a factory for what I do and I like Oliver, especially with the college here."

"It's a labor of love, isn't it?" She looked at a half-carved block of curly maple on the second workbench. It was already recognizable as a cello back. "Do you do it all by hand?"

"Almost. We have a drill, and a bench grinder. Unfortunately, my band saw broke down. That was useful. But that cello over there is all handmade. I have a very promising young man working with me. That's his, and it's going to be a beauty."

"Would that be Daniel Petris?"

"That's right. You know Daniel?"

"We've met."

"Very steady hand with a knife, Daniel has. He made me the best knife I ever had. Wonderful blade." He held it up as she would hold a pencil. She admired the grain and varnish of the handle and then watched with a sickening feeling as he demonstrated the wicked-looking angled blade on a scrap of the curly maple.

"Don't you ever cut yourself?" she made herself ask.

"This kind of work you have to do very precisely."

"But it's sharp enough?"

"It could cut you to the bone if you slipped." He looked at her quizzically. "Are you planning to take up violin making?"

"Oh, no. I was just wondering."

She continued to wonder all the way home.

# Chapter Seventeen

The Oliver Civic Symphony was turning out to be a churchgoing lot, unless maybe they played golf. The bright blue, almost October weather would tempt anyone.

Fred's elbow on the car's windowsill caught a perfect blend of sun and cool morning breeze. From time to time he passed a jogger; otherwise the streets were quiet. The hills of nearby Brown County, he knew, would already be swarming with tourists eager for a first glimpse of spectacular fall color. He looked down Prospect Avenue. An old maple that had survived a stroke of lightning a few years back was brilliant all down the injured side. Deep purple mixed with yellow and green on the sweet gums. Sassafras mittens were turning golden, and dogwood leaves and berries a bright red. A giant sycamore was shedding leaves the size of dinner plates.

It's all in your press agent, he thought.

No one had been home at the last three homes. Now it looked as if he might be wasting his time at the Wades', too; only a spanking new powder blue Cadillac faced him from the double garage. Then he remembered hearing Evelyn say in Werner's lab that Sam's Mercedes was in the shop. He might be home after all.

Sam, wearing Levis and an Izod shirt, opened the door.

"Something come up?" he asked.

"No, just routine. I'm looking for background information on Wanda Borowski. You're a witness in this one, Sam."

"Come on in."

He entered through a slate foyer. An antique umbrella stand stood ready at his left. Ahead, a sizable fig tree basked in the golden glow of the sun beaming down through a skylight.

There was nothing understated about the elegance of the living room. Fred's feet sank into deeply padded carpet. The Cadillac's pale blue appeared here in velvet chairs and satin draperies. Clutter was conspicuously absent. In a crystal vase, one perfect red rose was unfolding its first petals. He was sure the decorator would have approved.

"Have a seat," Sam said. "Coffee?"

"No, thanks." Fred outlined quickly his thinking about the relationship between Saturday's obvious murder and the nebulous question of George Petris.

"It wouldn't hold up in court, I know," he said. "Even so, I'm convinced that there's more than coincidence here. I'm worried, especially for those of you in the orchestra who were close to Petris. We don't need another Borowski."

"You're going house to house warning people?" Sam sounded faintly amused.

"Something like that. Go ahead, laugh. I'm not laughing, though, and I'd appreciate your help."

"I'll do what I can. Fire away." Sam draped an arm over a velvet cushion and leaned back elegantly.

"Let's stick with Borowski for a minute. What do you know about her?"

"Hardly anything. She was kind of quiet, didn't talk much about anything but the music. She played very well."

"Was she close to anyone in the orchestra? Did she have any enemies?"

"I don't know. I really didn't get to know her."

"How about Petris? I hear he was quite a womanizer."

"She wasn't his type."

"What was his type?"

"Not mousy. That's it, she was mousy."

"How come she had his oboe?"

"She caught it when he fell. I grabbed him and she grabbed it. When we saw how bad he was, she told him she'd take care of it, and he kind of nodded. That was that."

"You know it's missing."

Sam nodded. "I read it in the police report."

"Sam, would an oboe be worth much on the open market? Was there anything special about this one? It seems like an unlikely think to walk off with."

"It's a good instrument, a Lorée, pretty much the twin of mine, although no two are ever quite the same. They depreciate. It might bring fifteen hundred or thereabouts, if you could find the right buyer. You couldn't fence it. The serial number would have a trail a mile wide. Nothing else was stolen?"

"No," Fred said. "It's a funny business."

"I suppose she didn't have much worth taking. I had the impression that she lived fairly simply."

"There was some cash lying around, and antique silver right there in the buffet."

"That's funny, all right." Sam's forehead wrinkled. "You think she surprised a sneak thief before he could take off with the goods, and he killed her and ran with the first thing handy?"

"No. She spent the whole morning at home. The kids and the neighbors agree about that. There's another possibility, though. We still haven't recovered the weapon, and if this was a spur of the moment thing, I wonder if it wasn't the reed knife. Petris did have one, didn't he?"

"Oh, sure."

"I can't remember what they look like. Is yours handy?"

Sam patted his pockets and handed Fred a black-handled knife, its blade covered by a brown leatherette case with a metal rim.

Fred whistled softly when he removed the case. Three inches long and almost an inch wide, the blade tapered from a back an eighth of an inch across to an edge as sharp as any razor's. He found the gap where the blade entered the plastic handle too dark to see how solidly it was seated.

"I'd think one of these would have no trouble doing the job," he said, testing the edge cautiously with his thumb. "The handle would give us decent prints, too, if we got lucky enough to find it. Okay to show this to Henshaw?"

Sam shrugged. "I won't need it till Wednesday."

"Wednesday?" Fred sheathed the blade and pocketed the knife.

"Orchestra night. Far as I know, we're rehearsing."

"I'll want to be there."

"Don't you think you're carrying this orchestra bit a little far? Sure you aren't just interested in that Mrs. Spencer?"

"Where did you get that idea?"

"Catherine Turner catered the dinner Friday. It was one of those stand-up deals. Don't ever go into politics, Fred. There comes a time when your arm drops off from shaking hands, your teeth are dying of exposure, and you can hear your stomach rumbling during what passes for dinner. I finally sneaked out to the kitchen and intercepted a tray of hot things straight from the oven. I almost didn't get away. Catherine and I go way back, and she had a few choice things to say about you and Mrs. Spencer."

"There's nothing to say." Fred tried to keep his voice light. Inside, he fumed. Who did Catherine think she was, staking out a claim on him like that, and to the county attorney?

"That's not the way she heard it. Her Aunt Trudie says you made a date with the lady."

"I don't even know her Aunt Trudie."

"Maybe not, but she knew you when you came into the Senior Citizens' Center. Better watch your step. Catherine was spittin' nails."

That explained the uproar about the sourdough on Saturday. Fred had no intention of becoming Catherine's exclusive property and even less of discussing the matter.

"Speaking of food, Sam, I've been wondering how many wind players eat before they play."

"I always have supper."

"I was thinking of the refreshments at the orchestra break."

"You're really taking this poisoning business seriously, aren't you?" Fred didn't answer.

"All right, all right. Me, I stick to water. Anything else gunks up the instrument."

"That's what my old band director always tried to tell us at football games. You can imagine how well we listened. How about Petris and Borowski?"

"They both kept away from crumbs, too, but I think he usually had whatever they were offering to drink. I'm not sure about her. It didn't seem to affect his playing any."

"Good, was he?"

"We were lucky to have him as a player." A large "but" hung there, unspoken.

"And otherwise?"

"I got along with him all right. I'm sure you've heard by now that he'd never win a popularity contest."

"Any of the other folks who knew about reed knives likely to have it in for him—or for Borowski?"

"I still think you're barking up the wrong tree." Sam stood up. "Tell you what, Fred. Go talk it over with the little Mrs. Spencer. You wouldn't want to make a liar out of Aunt Trudie, would you?"

Fred accepted the pleasantry as the dismissal it was. At the door, he turned back for one last question.

"Almost forgot, Sam. Where were you between ten o'clock and noon yesterday?"

The politician's smile held.

"In and out of the office. Maxine keeps a log."

"Thanks. See you Wednesday, if not before."

He decided to give Elmer Rush another try before stopping for a late lunch. As he pulled up in front of the house, he saw the wheelchair halfway down the block and went on foot to meet it.

♩♩♩

Rush remembered him from his visit to the Senior Citizens' Center. Frowning, he introduced Julie in a friendly enough tone.

"Mr. Lundquist is a policeman, Julie," he told her.

Her smile made Fred wish he could add a dozen of his excess years to her mental ones. He held out his hand.

"Hello, Julie. How are you?"

"Fine." She beamed at him and took his hand as a small child would.

"I met Julie's mother," he said over her head. "She explained about her. Sounds like a freak accident."

"Accident, my foot!" Rush exploded. "It was criminal. Someone had been fooling with the safety grill over the pool's filter. Julie must have dislodged it, and the suction of the pump held her underwater. By the time I finally got the so-called lifeguard to turn it off, the bruise on her back was the shape of the drain."

Julie was beginning to look back and forth at their troubled faces. Her own mouth turned down.

"But now you're just fine, aren't you, punkin?" her grandfather said quickly, giving the wheelchair a twirl. She giggled, sounding like any little girl on a merry-go-round.

"What can I do for you, Lieutenant?" Rush asked, maintaining the light tone he had just used with Julie.

"It's about Mrs. Borowski."

"Mrs. who?"

"She played flute in the symphony."

"I don't know her."

"Maybe you read about her or heard it on the news. She was murdered yesterday."

"I saw the story, but I didn't read it. Those things depress me." He gripped the chair and marched it toward the house. Fred's long strides kept up easily.

"I don't want to upset you, but I do hope you can help me with a couple of things. Would you rather wait until Julie's home?"

"If you must."

They left Julie with her mother and continued walking. As soon as they were out of earshot, Rush turned on Fred.

"What business did you have bothering my daughter?"

"I was looking for you."

"You were dredging up old horror stories. There's no call for that." Grim-faced, he marched on, his back straight and his every step a slap at the pavement.

"No, there wouldn't be. I mentioned to Mrs. Lambert that I had seen you at the Senior Citizens' Center with Julie. She told me less than you did about what happened to her."

"You called it a freak accident."

"Mr. Rush, I've seen a lot of drownings. It's a rare thing that someone survives after being under long enough to have problems from it, and it was even less common some years back. I'm sorry it happened to Julie. She's a beautiful young woman."

"What did you want with me?" He wasn't yielding an inch.

"As I said, I'm investigating the death of Wanda Borowski. She was the flute player who sat almost immediately in front of you in the symphony rehearsal last Wednesday—the one who packed up the oboe when George Petris became ill."

"Oh, her." Rush scratched the top of his ear. "I don't know what I could tell you about her."

"What about him? I didn't want to alarm your daughter, but there is some question about his death, too. We're considering the possibility that Mrs. Borowski might have been killed because she was in a position to notice something before he died."

"That's pretty far-fetched."

"I hope so. If not, I'm afraid you might be in some danger yourself."

"Oh." They took a few steps in silence. "I can't think of anything. I really think you'd do better to talk to people who knew him longer."

"I understand that you and he had become fairly friendly by last Wednesday."

"All I did was set out to make a little peace. I see no point in playing in a group like that if there's constant backbiting."

"Backbiting?"

"I don't know what that man's problem was, but I learned a long time ago that the best way to win someone over is to ask his advice. I've been winding reeds since before he was born, so I let him teach me how to do it. Never fails." His eyes suddenly twinkled.

Fred ran through the details of the rehearsal and the break. Rush had gone out for some cool air, but he hadn't bothered with the punch and cookies nor taken particular notice of those who had.

"I drank that stuff the week before and wished I hadn't. This old dog learns fast." He grinned. His anger seemed to have disappeared completely. Fred was beginning to understand what Martha Lambert had meant about her father's moods. They turned the corner at the end of the block.

"Did you notice anything unusual about the oboe itself?"

"No, I was paying more attention to the man. Then I was packing up."

"Just for the record, can you remember where you were yesterday morning, say between ten and noon?"

"Home. Martha took the other kids out shopping. I stayed with Julie."

"Would she remember that, if I asked her?"

"There's no point in bothering Julie. She'd remember anything I told her to—for a little while, anyway. One day's the same as another to Julie."

More questioning yielded nothing useful. Fred finally had to content himself with warning the old man again.

"Don't worry, Lieutenant." The fire was back in the faded blue eyes. "When I got the golden handshake at sixty-five, I didn't think I'd ever be needed again, but Martha and Julie need me now. I'm not going to let anything more happen to that child. *Nobody* is going to take me away from my family."

I hope not, Fred thought.

# Chapter Eighteen

Reaching for the phone to call Fred, Joan jumped when it rang. For a moment she thought he had read her mind, but it was only Yoichi, asking apologetically whether she would be willing to copy some bowings on string parts he had just received from Alex.

"They came in the mail yesterday and she doesn't want to use any rehearsal time," he explained. "She has marked the first stands' parts; we won't have to work for the score."

Joan thought personally that violin sectionals would save more time in rehearsal than anything she and Yoichi could put on paper, but she felt too much like the new kid on the block to suggest such a thing. Other people's behavior during rehearsal suggested that Alex had been wasting their time for years.

"Can you bring them over?"

"It will take some time. The bicycle is not working properly. I think something is wrong with the gears."

"Do you think that's why you fell?"

"I don't know. I am not very mechanical. I will take it to be repaired tomorrow."

There went any chance of practicing today. Her own laundry awaited her, and the dozen small chores she now put off until weekends. Still, a thousand a year was worth some minor inconvenience. She wrote down his address and promised to arrive before suppertime.

She reached Fred on her second try and told him as succinctly as she could about Daniel's prowess with sharp knives and about Yoichi's fall and bloody sweater.

"How does he look?" Fred asked.

"I don't know. I'll see him soon. I'm leaving to pick up some music from him."

"Not alone, you're not. I'll meet you in ten minutes. I want to see for myself."

If Yoichi was startled when they arrived together, he managed not to show it. He thanked Joan for her advice. The sweater, he said, was like new. Dividing up the parts, he gave Joan the seconds and violas to mark, and kept the firsts and cellos for himself.

Joan saw with a sinking heart that the music was Rezniek's overture to *Donna Diana*, whose soaring theme once heralded the grueling radio adventures of Sergeant Preston of the Yukon.

For her, however, it evoked instantly a nightmarish summer high school music camp at which she had been the sole violist, faced with a long series of arpeggios filled with accidentals that demanded rapid string crossings and forays into half and second positions, all at a tempo beyond what she could manage. It wasn't a solo—the oboe had the melody—but only the viola part supplied that tricky underpinning, and only Joan had registered to play viola that session.

She had spent most of her practice time on the dreaded passage, bringing it to a shaky adequacy at the last minute. Briefly, the weight of the world had been lifted from her shoulders by the arrival of a "ringer" from a nearby music school for the dress rehearsal and final concert. It had crashed down on her again when, the first time through the overture, the music student had told her quietly, "You're on your own. I'm going to have to fake this one. I'd never get it right with only one rehearsal." All these years later, just seeing the music could still start her adrenaline flowing. Maybe the new kid could suggest a viola sectional, she thought. At least I won't be alone this time.

Yoichi was responding to Fred's friendly questions about his accident. No, he hadn't been hurt badly enough to need a doctor. He had been riding to the grocery, he said, but he'd postponed his shopping and returned home instead to clean up.

"What time did all this happen?" The question was still friendly, but Joan wondered how Yoichi could possibly miss its purpose.

"Eleven o'clock. I heard the chimes on the college square before I fell." He smiled, a little stiffly because of the crusted-over place on his left cheek, but his eyes didn't meet the big detective's.

"Were you leaving from home?"

"Yes, I was studying here in the morning."

"Alone?"

"Yes. I can't prove it. What time did she die?"

No flies on him, Joan thought.

"We're working on that," Fred answered, still friendly. "Thank you for your help."

In one fluid motion Yoichi knelt to retrieve a violin part that had slipped to the floor. He reminded Joan to use a soft pencil and to mark the bowings lightly.

"Alex may change her mind, or the concertmaster. I hope she consulted him this time. I think he sometimes makes changes only to show that he is concertmaster. Not always good ones." He smiled, but Joan was sure he meant it.

On the way back, Fred was quiet. Pulling up in front of Joan's house, he said, "I wish I could believe him. His face is scraped about right for a fall."

"But?"

"Did you see him pick that music off the floor? You told me he was stiff and sore."

"He's probably more accustomed to kneeling than we are. Besides, how do you know it didn't hurt?"

"I can't put my finger on it. I always have the feeling that he's holding something back."

She avoided his eyes.

"You, too?" he asked. She laughed.

"No, that was an experiment. The sweater business made me wonder and I don't really know him at all. But I do know not to worry that he doesn't look me in the eye. That's not Japanese. Yoichi has been here for some time, you can tell, but under stress I suspect he'll always come across as shifty-eyed if you don't know better."

"Could be. Humor me, though—don't spend any time alone with him. I'll be there Wednesday night, by the way. I'm talking with individual members today, but I think I'd better see a rehearsal."

"'See' is right. It's much too early to listen. We're still awfully ragged."

After he left, she flicked through the music. The fearsome stretch jumped out at her. She could imagine the cutting remarks from the oboe section—but no, not this week. Still, a knot twisted somewhere in the middle when she thought of the speed at which Alex would probably take those unending broken chords. She set the marked viola part on her stand, and tossed the others and the seconds into the box of orchestra folders. The bowings could wait.

When Andrew arrived home, she was woodshedding away and not inclined to stop. She'd already put in so many fingerings that she knew she'd have to label another copy Viola 1 and keep this one for herself. Maybe John Hocking wouldn't mind playing from it and she wouldn't have to remember what she'd worked out. She was pleased to find that she knew the key changes solidly, at least in her ears. Unfortunately, memory hadn't carried over to her fingers at all. If Alex would show a little mercy on the tempo, though, she thought she might manage something more than pure faking by Wednesday.

"What's for supper?" Andrew asked, tossing his books on the sofa.

"I don't know. Surprise me." She dug into another six-note pattern, first repeating it over and over, and then connecting it to those before and after it. It was the changes that threw her, and the lack of let-up.

"You're really messing up," Andrew said.

Joan repressed a snarl.

"Andrew, can you say 'rubber baby buggy bumpers'?"

"Rubber baby buggy bumpers. Why?"

"Now say it ten times, fast."

"Come on, Mom."

"Go ahead, try."

He survived three before degenerating into "bubby bunkers" and retreating into the kitchen, where she could hear him slamming doors and muttering to himself. Half an hour later, she was willing to call a truce with the overture. She wiped the excess rosin off the strings and laid the viola in its case. Andrew appeared in the doorway.

"Which omelet do you want, Mom, the one with onion or the plain cheese?"

It wasn't a joke. He had managed two perfectly browned omelets, light and moist in the middle. The coffee was hot, the toast crisp, and the salad fresh.

"Who taught you to make an omelet?" Joan asked, after the first forkful of the cheese. "This is wonderful."

"It is, isn't it?" he said between bites. "I think I have a natural gift. I should cook more often."

"That could be arranged. What else can you do?"

"Depends on what's in the refrigerator. Ham, turkey, mushrooms—combinations. Almost did a turkey-cheese-onion tonight, but we were out of turkey."

"All omelets?"

"You don't like omelets?" His face was innocence itself.

"Love 'em," she said firmly. "I'll probably die young, full of cholesterol, but with a smile on my face."

♮♮♮

She was telling Margaret Duffy about it while they pitched in to fold mimeographed newsletters after the Senior Citizens' Center board meeting on Monday morning.

"He keeps surprising me. I'm enjoying him and I don't think I'm cramping his style too much."

"You probably give him the kind of freedom your folks gave you. I'll tell you, the Zimmermans set this town on its ear with their notions about bringing up children."

"Notions? My parents?"

"I'll never forget the night they took on the PTA over the issue of corporal punishment. There was some disagreement about what teachers should be allowed to do to other people's children, but your parents went out on a limb all by themselves when they said in public that they didn't spank their own."

"They never mentioned it at home," Joan said.

"Probably not, but the teachers' lounge buzzed for a week about how you'd turn out."

"And then we left town before they could find out. I wonder what they'd think if they knew I was a Zimmerman."

"Well, it did come up when you applied for this job."

"It didn't!" She stopped folding in surprise. "And they hired me."

"Alvin Hannauer didn't hurt. He was tickled to have your father on the dig that year. Experienced anthropologists didn't drop in every day, you know, especially not with a grant in hand to study Rattlesnake Mound. Mostly he had to manage with students who wanted him to pay them while he tried to teach them not to destroy all the evidence every time they discovered an artifact."

Joan chuckled. "He sounds just like Dad."

"They had a lot in common," Margaret said. "Anyway, when the board was dragging its feet about you—you didn't have the qualifications on paper, and even worse, you were a stranger—Alvin said he'd heard about you in letters for years and we'd be lucky to get you."

Touched to know that her usually uncommunicative father had written anything about her at all, much less letters with such an effect, Joan was grateful to the man who had spoken up for her.

"I'll have to thank him. I didn't think anybody but you would know about me."

"Well, of course, I didn't, not really," Margaret said. "Not the way I know the people I watch grow up around here. I taught two generations of quite a few families—three of some."

Of course. Margaret would know Oliver inside out.

"You probably taught a lot of the people in the orchestra, didn't you?" Joan asked, reaching for a stack of mailing labels.

"Well, yes, over the years. Most of them left town. It's amazing how little the ones who stayed have changed, though. Nancy Krebs never listened in class and she's still too wound up in her own affairs to hear what anyone else has to say. Makes for boring conversation."

Trust Margaret Duffy to put her finger on it.

"Nancy says Evelyn Wade was in our class, too, but I don't remember her."

"You and Evelyn didn't see much of each other. She was a bossy little thing—spoiled rotten, I thought. But that sounds like a whiny child and she never whined. Still, when she set out after something, she was accustomed to getting it and she always made it show. She was big on show—used to draw little circles over all the i's in her schoolwork but couldn't be bothered about spelling. You were just the opposite. Pigtails and shoelaces always coming undone. I expect she would have looked down on you, if you'd noticed her. But you went around with your nose in a book and missed half the snubs that came your way."

"I remember enough." Joan resisted the temptation to check her back hair. "Did you teach Wanda Borowski or George Petris?"

"I taught Daniel and Emily Petris. The parents came from somewhere on the West Coast. Emily followed her mother back there when that marriage broke up. Daniel floated around Oliver like a lost soul for a year or two, but he seems to have pulled himself together recently."

"Probably because of Mr. Isaac." Joan described her visit to the violin studio and Isaac's obvious pride in the beautiful cello back Daniel was carving. She caught herself before mentioning anything about knives, even to Margaret, although it seemed a laughable precaution. Instead, she asked about Wanda.

"Yes, I remember Wanda," Margaret said. "She came to me fresh from St. Paul's. I often wondered whether she'd become a nun herself."

"Why?"

"I don't know. I suppose it was because she was so meticulous in everything she did. She was quiet, never boisterous, seemed almost afraid of boys. Five years in all-girl classes might account for that, but it didn't have that effect on most of the girls. But I was wrong."

"Maybe you weren't that far off. Her house felt like a convent to me. Old-fashioned, painfully clean. I remember wondering if the children were ever allowed to mess things up. And she planned ahead. At eleven in the morning, she had supper going in a slow cooker, and I think she must have sprinkled those shirts the night before or at the crack of dawn, they were so evenly damp. It felt like the old nursery rhyme: 'This is the day we iron our shirts.'"

"Old habits die hard, Joan. There was a time I thought the world would come to an end if I washed on Saturday instead of Monday, but what else could a schoolteacher do? Of course, back then it took all day—you couldn't just toss a few things into the automatic when you wanted them. But I still organize my life that way. Only now it's Saturday that feels like the only right day, even as long as I've been retired."

Joan was sitting very still, her fingers idle.

"Joan, are you all right?"

She came to life slowly.

"I'm sorry, Margaret, did you say something? I wasn't tuned in. I think…I think I've just figured something out."

# Chapter Nineteen

A cup of Monday morning coffee at his elbow, Fred hunched over his desk in the windowless squadroom sifting through a fat stack of reports on the Borowski murder and his own skimpy notes on the Petris case.

The poisoned cup, he was convinced, had been burned with the rest of the trash. The only angle he could see on George Petris was the possibility that the killer considered Wanda Borowski a threat, and he knew he was swimming upstream on that. He hadn't been pulled off the case, but he could feel the stifled snickers when his back was turned.

I'm paranoid, he told himself, and turned to the reports. Still no weapon. All the Borowski kitchen knives were clean as the proverbial whistle. Whoever coined that expression had spent precious little time with wind instruments, he thought. They all smelled of spit sooner or later. Clean or not, though, George's oboe hadn't been turned up by an exhaustive search of the Borowskis' neighborhood.

Isaac had sworn that none of his knives had left the violin studio, which was locked on Saturday. It mattered very little, after all. Daniel might have made a knife of his own—he'd shown his talent in that direction. Or, like anyone else arriving at Wanda's house when she had the oboe waiting for him, he might have used his father's missing reed knife. Fred picked up the phone to check with the pathologist about the knife Sam had lent him Sunday.

"Just saw it," Dr. Henshaw answered, much too cheerfully for a Monday morning. "Sure, it would make a clean cut like that. Too bad the end of the blade is rounded off, though. Give me a nice wedge-shaped end, now, and I might be able to match it to a mark that would pin it down."

"You found a mark?" This was news.

"No, but if I had."

If we had some ham, we could have ham and eggs, Fred thought gloomily, if we had some eggs.

"Okay if I send it back with the kitchen knives?" Henshaw asked.

"As long as it's here Wednesday."

"No problem."

Fred turned back to the reports. Although he had kept the time of Wanda's death out of the paper, there was little mystery about it. The old ladies had seen her alive and apparently well at ten-thirty, and Fred himself had recorded the call from Daniel Petris at eleven. It stretched credulity to picture Daniel first making that call and then murdering the lady. Besides, Henshaw had put the time of death at not later than eleven, and they had run the washing machine through its cycle. Working back from the time Joan heard it stop, Fred estimated that Wanda must have started that last load no earlier than ten minutes to eleven. Sometime in those ten minutes, then, someone had walked into her house unobserved, killed her without rousing the neighbors, and left without leaving so much as a footprint in the blood that splattered the bedroom floor and puddled around her body.

So it was going to come down to the tedium of ten-minute alibis. He gave a copy of the orchestra personnel list to Kyle Pruitt and explained what he wanted.

"Hate to do this to you, son."

"You really think one of them in the orchestra cut her?" The young sergeant's eagerness reminded him of his own at the same age. With a round face, red hair, and a toothy grin, Pruitt looked a little too much like a plump version of the "What, me worry?" kid to be taken seriously in plain clothes. A former high school linebacker, he now resembled a budding sumo wrestler more than a lean, hard cop, and he knew it.

"I don't know, but it's time to start weeding out the ones who couldn't have." Fred borrowed the paper back and made little checks by the names of Elmer Rush and Yoichi Nakamura. "I've already talked to these two."

"You sure you want me to talk to Wade?" asked Kyle, always leery of the bureaucrats.

"Just check with his secretary. They were working Saturday."

"And the ladies?" Kyle's big forefinger indicated the members of the symphony guild.

"Mrs. Wallston and Mrs. Wade were at the rehearsal when Petris died. I think you can skip the others for now. And, Kyle..." He paused.

"Sir?"

"Anybody can't tell you where he was, you just say thanks anyway and leave. The polite cop, that's you. All I want this time out are the easy answers."

"Take their word for it?"

"Get all the confirmation you can. Just don't pick a fight to do it."

Kyle blushed as only a redhead can. It hadn't been an idle reminder. That eagerness had landed him in hot water more than once. He left, looking somewhat subdued. Fred hoped the mood would last.

He was a little curious to know how long it would take for the word to get around that the police were connecting Borowski and Petris. Not that Kyle Pruitt would be saying any such thing. He was to approach the members of the orchestra as people who knew the victim of a brutal murder and to ask whether they had seen her the morning she was killed. Routine questions about possible enemies or reasons someone might have had for killing her would lead up to a last-minute turn and a casual "By the way, where were you Saturday between ten and twelve?" If Kyle managed the approach skillfully enough, he might not have to ask the question at all. All things considered, however, Fred gave the Oliver grapevine an hour at most.

♭♮♯

Forty minutes later, the desk sergeant buzzed him with the news that a young woman wanted to make a statement about the Borowski murder.

"Who is she?"

"Name of Lisa Wallston."

"Send her in. No, I'll come for her."

Fred threaded his way through the maze of desks and corridors to the front. Daniel Petris had called her good-looking. He hadn't said she was a knockout. Slender, blond, with summer's tan still warm on her skin, Lisa filled her trim slacks and simple cotton blouse in all the right places. The longest, darkest lashes he'd ever seen on a face untouched by cosmetics fringed her surprising brown eyes. She turned them on him full force, with no trace of a smile.

"Detective Lundquist?"

"Miss Wallston." They shook hands.

"I've come to tell you about Daniel."

He led her back to an empty office, aware as she surely must be of the heads turning in their direction. She gave no sign of noticing. He supposed she must be used to it. Nevertheless, he pulled the door half shut. He swiveled his chair toward hers, leaned back, and hooked his toes under the desk drawer.

"So, tell me about Daniel. You do mean Daniel Petris?"

"The whole town knows I mean Daniel Petris. Where have you been?" Her accent was soft Hoosier, but her voice had a hard edge he wasn't altogether sure he believed.

He waited. She glared at him.

"They say you're asking where people were yesterday morning, when that woman was killed."

"That's right."

"Daniel was with me. I don't know what he said—he maybe didn't want to drag me into this—but we spent the night in my apartment. I'm surprised the busybodies haven't already told you." She challenged him to make something of it.

"When did he leave?" Fred asked, not rising to the bait.

"Noon, maybe. I'm not exactly sure." She tucked a long strand of straight blond hair back behind her right ear.

"You mean you're not sure when she was killed."

"No, that's not what I mean at all." She bristled.

"You haven't talked to him."

"Not since Saturday." Now she was beginning to hedge.

"Miss Wallston, I might as well tell you. We know Daniel was at the Borowskis' house by eleven Saturday morning." He tilted his chair upright and leaned toward her. "Why did you come?"

All the starch had gone out of her. Suddenly she shrugged and smiled, dazzlingly.

"I guess I thought he was worth it. I couldn't let him get messed up in something like this." The smile faded. "Daniel didn't kill that woman, I know he didn't."

"Maybe not, but you didn't help him any—or yourself, for that matter."

"So it was dumb. I've done worse things. He didn't deserve them either. Only this time I was trying to help."

"Why did you think Daniel might be involved? His name hasn't been mentioned."

"But I thought..." Lisa stopped in some confusion. The hair escaped from behind her ear. She pushed it back.

"You thought?" Fred prompted.

"I thought you thought the person who killed George killed this Mrs. Borowski, too."

The grapevine wins again. "And you thought Daniel killed his father, is that it?"

"N-no." She backpedaled rapidly. "I don't know what I thought. I just know Daniel is twice the man his father ever was. George talked a wonderful line, but he never lived up to an obligation in his life. He flunked fatherhood, made a mess out of his marriage, and wrecked my life. I'm not sorry he's dead and I won't pretend to be."

"I understand your mother was serving refreshments at the rehearsal the night he died."

"Was she?" She stopped short. "You don't think for a minute my mother would kill a man! Why, she's a nurse," she said, as if that made all the difference.

"Do you know where she was Saturday morning?"

"She was working. I was home. That part was true." She pushed the hair back again, her fingers following the curve of her ear. "Daniel didn't spend the night. I haven't seen him or his crummy father for months."

"Any neighbors around? Anybody see you?"

"No."

"Phone calls?"

"No."

Fred added her to his list of unconfirmed alibis. True, she hadn't been anywhere near Petris during the rehearsal, but her mother had. And although it would be easy to check whether her mother had been on duty Saturday, Lisa herself might have been anywhere. Together, they had opportunity—and undeniable motive, if the second murder was in some way to cover the first. From what he'd seen at Werner's lab, access to the poison wouldn't have been a problem for anyone who knew what to look for. For that matter, hadn't the aquarium man said something about salamanders and Lisa? Hers had all died. Maybe her mother had helped them along.

All along, he'd been wondering why Glenda Wallston would be willing to be in the same room as the man who had ruined her daughter's life. In his early rash of phone calls, one of Lisa's busybodies had suggested that Glenda was struggling with her Christian duty to forgive and avoid judging George Petris. A little hard to forgive a man you haven't judged, he thought, but he knew he was splitting hairs. Real forgiveness would be asking a good deal. And whether or not Glenda herself would have killed Wanda, who had done her no wrong, he had no trouble seeing Lisa impetuously rush in to protect her mother from suspicion. Glenda might not even have known about the second murder.

As Wanda's killer, Lisa would know Daniel to be innocent but not know that he had followed her to the Borowski house so closely as to disprove her lie on his behalf. Fred decided to let her stew in her own juice for a while, whatever her reason for lying. He walked her back to the door, ignoring as she did the looks that came their way.

At the blind corner that was the scene of countless spilled cups of coffee, they collided with three men who were as oblivious to Lisa as she was to them. Kyle Pruitt recovered first, but not even he gave her more than an automatic apology. Captain Warren Altschuler, chief of detectives, didn't bother.

"My office, Lundquist," he said over his shoulder. "Come in, Sam."

# Chapter Twenty

Fred followed Sam Wade into the captain's office. The door closed in Kyle Pruitt's face, but not on his mouth, Fred was sure. The whole squadroom would know what was up before he did.

He was wrong.

"Just what do you think you're doing, sending Pruitt to grill my secretary?" Sam exploded. "I got there this morning and found myself murder suspect number one, with the whole staff drinking it in."

"What's this all about, Fred?" Altschuler asked, somewhat more mildly. "I told Sam this was the first I'd heard he was under suspicion of any kind."

Fred looked down at the stocky, pug-nosed captain, his homely face the antithesis of Sam's polished good looks.

"He's not. Just what did Pruitt say?"

"It wasn't what he said, it was what he did. He had Maxine going through her log for Saturday morning, accounting for every ten minutes of Sam's time. What was he even doing in that office?"

Fred sighed. Kyle himself had known better. I should have listened to him, he thought.

"Making a mountain out of a molehill, it sounds like. We've narrowed the Borowski murder down to a ten-minute period. I sent him out with a list of orchestra personnel to thin out the possibles. We even rehearsed what he'd say to the players before asking them about times, but I guess he knew better than to try to snow Maxine. Besides, he knew Sam already told us what he could about Petris and Borowski. He was just there to confirm it." He gritted his teeth. "I'm sorry if he made it into a major scene. Kyle gets a little carried away sometimes. I'll talk to him."

The apology cost him something, even though every word was true.

He intercepted an exchange of glances between the chief and the prosecutor. At Sam's almost imperceptible nod, Altschuler let fly.

"Let's get something straight and let's get it straight right now. We are seriously undermanned and we all know that the Petris thing is a crock. I left you on Borowski because you'd already spent time on the kid who called it in. Maybe the husband killed her, maybe the kid killed her, I don't know. What I do know is that you're grasping at straws to make connections with this crazy idea about the orchestra. Forget it. Stick to Borowski. I want some solid facts and I want them soon. Is that clear?"

It was clear, all right. So clear that something inside Fred snapped and the resentment he'd been swallowing for years poured over him. He was the dumb Democrat Swede to be passed over for promotions. Lundquist the has-been, hanging onto press clippings as if they meant something. Good enough for crocks, not crooks. Ready for the golden handshake Elmer Rush had resented.

"Oh, sure." He didn't bother to disguise the bitterness he felt. "It's clear. You want me to blow it, so you can say I don't have what it takes anymore. But as long as I'm on the force, I'm going to give it my damnedest, no matter what you think.

"You both asked me to check out Nakamura's fish story. And now that I've got some evidence it's not so crazy after all, you say forget it. If I forget Petris, I might as well forget Borowski. As far as I'm concerned, everybody in the room when Petris collapsed is a suspect in both cases. Not the only ones, by a long shot, but the best ones I have right now."

He'd been looking from one man to the other. Now he turned to Altschuler.

"Why you want me to avoid clearing Sam I can't imagine," he said. "I always thought you two were on the same side of the fence. But what do I know? You want me to leave him on the list or you want to get the hell out of my way and let me work?"

He towered over Altschuler, who stood up to the onslaught without flinching, but the chief's answering glare flickered briefly, and Fred saw Sam's eyes rolling wearily toward the ceiling. Humor him, the eyes said. Or maybe it was, Oh God, there goes the hothead again. Altschuler's mouth was moving.

"...blown out of all proportion. I have great respect for your abilities, Fred, you know that. But sending Pruitt on a routine check is like going after flies with an elephant swatter. If you really think all this legwork is necessary, take Ketcham. He'll cover twice the ground in half the time."

Older and subtler, Ketcham would have been Fred's choice in the first place.

"All right," he said, his heart still pounding. "Do I have to clear every move he makes with the prosecuting attorney's office?"

Sam reached out a conciliatory hand. "I'll tell Maxine to relax. You have my full support."

And I'll want yours on election day, that's the rest of the speech. Fred fought down his anger and returned the obligatory handshake.

At his desk a few minutes later, a dozen retorts he might have made crowded into his mind, followed immediately by some of the things he actually had said. The early retirement that had looked so tempting only a week or so before suddenly loomed as disciplinary action—another thing altogether. Dumb Swede, he told himself. Now look what you've done. Sam's "full support," he suspected, would hold up only until some fat cat political contributor squawked at being questioned.

He called Kyle Pruitt over, told him bluntly that he'd been replaced, and asked how far he'd made it down the list before hitting the prosecutor's office.

Pruitt's face was bright pink. "I'm real sorry about that," he said. "That Maxine tore into me so loud, the whole office heard her."

"It happens. What did you learn?"

"I found these two," Kyle said, pointing to the first two viola players, who according to Joan's lopsided map sat immediately in front of the oboes. "They both give violin lessons to little kids all Saturday morning. No breaks. Parents sit in. I got the names of the kids who were there from ten-thirty until eleven-thirty."

"Good. If we're lucky, there will be more like them. What else?"

"Then I ran into Maxine."

"Did she tell you anything?"

"Oh, sure. Wade's clear. She logs the people in that office within an inch of their lives. They say over there she knows more than God. That's what got her so mad. She wanted me to take her word for it, but I made her show me the log. Wade came over here at ten-fifteen Saturday and she logged him back in at ten-fifty-eight. According to our desk, he left here at half past ten."

"And his car was in the shop Saturday," Fred said. "Not that he might not have walked anyway." They both knew that Sam Wade preached physical fitness. Kyle had been the recipient of more than one sermon on the subject. Even Sam's brisk pace, however, wouldn't have allowed him to kill Wanda Borowski at ten-fifty, mop up the blood, and arrive back in his office eight minutes later.

"Thanks, Kyle."

Fred sat for long minutes, drained but not relieved by his outburst. Being right didn't ease the almost physical pain of knowing how low he really ranked. A heaviness lodged itself under his breastbone, and the back of his throat tightened. For all his defiant words, he wanted nothing more than to curl up and quit.

Ketcham was out. Fred left him a note and took the personnel list, chiefly as an excuse to escape the building. Ethel Cykler, the second bassoonist, would complete the ring of players who had surrounded George Petris. Her address, 9799 North Alcorn Road, meant she lived several miles out of town. Rural residents were still complaining about the new post office regulation that had done away with rural route box numbers, but the police were discovering that street addresses greatly simplified the job of finding them at home. Come to think of it, he thought, maybe that's what they're complaining about.

Hillsides of yellow and green tipped with the flames of oaks and sugar maples and dotted with the deeper reds of sumac and dogwood lifted his spirits as he drove. When he caught himself whistling as if he'd just received a promotion instead of a dressing down, he resolved not to hurry back.

Joan's message lay unread on his cluttered desk.

# Chapter Twenty-One

Ethel Cykler, wearing only a red tank suit and hoop earrings, was pushing an old people-powered mower around the patchy grass in front of her ramshackle farmhouse. Stately maples and stumps of substantial elms testified to better days. Potatoes and onions lay drying in a garden bordered by rhubarb and asparagus fern. Guinea hens shrieked warning when Fred turned into the driveway.

He saw her look up, but she completed her circle around the yard, toes dug into the grass and stringy arm muscles straining. He waited in the car, shutting off the engine so that she'd know he wasn't merely using her drive as a convenient turnaround on the narrow gravel road. He hadn't seen a dog yet, but he wasn't taking any chances.

"Mrs. Cykler?" he called.

"Mother's dead. I'm Ethel," she answered, finally walking over to the car. He got out.

"Detective Lieutenant Lundquist, Oliver police. I'd appreciate a few minutes of your time."

"I've been looking for a reason to rest my feet," she said. "You'll do. Want some water?"

"Please."

They sat in hickory split chairs on the shady porch sipping well water as if it were mint juleps, she apparently unself-conscious in her bathing suit and calloused bare feet. Her skin was deeply tanned, her hair a mass of sweat-dampened gray curls plastered to her head. Skinny and hard, she had a face full of lines, whether from age or sun and wind he couldn't tell. Tough old bird, he thought, wondering whether he could come within a dozen years of guessing how old.

"Think you'll know me next time?" she asked sharply.

"Sorry." He felt his face go hot. "Habit, I guess," he said, knowing that it wasn't. A cop's habit sized people up quickly, rather than staring at them until they felt it.

She finished her water and began drumming her fingers on her knee, but he didn't want to get to his reason for coming. Maybe this was his reason, just the sitting on this porch, watching the leaves turn. He wrenched his thoughts back to that bloody room, back to the sturdy little girls who had comforted their father.

"Miss Cykler," he began.

"Ethel."

He nodded. "How well did you know Wanda Borowski?"

"Depends on what you mean by well. We saw each other every Wednesday night most weeks out of the past ten years. Played chamber music a few times. I can't say as I really knew her, but we were acquainted, don't you know. We weren't friends."

"Is that typical?"

"Of what?"

"Her, you, the orchestra—take your pick."

"Orchestra." She snorted. "I've played in that orchestra fifteen years this fall. Up to last week I would've called Alex Campbell a friend. Then Mr. Charming California walked in and took over. You want to know something? When a good-looking man comes along, never mind how old, friends aren't worth chicken feed. I found that out."

He nodded and sipped. It occurred to him that if Elmer Rush had been poisoned, Ethel would have been a prime candidate.

"Fifteen years and I'm right back to second bassoon. I almost walked out, but I wouldn't give her the satisfaction. Besides, the old coot can't hang on forever. I'll outlast him, you watch." She was breathing fire now. Interruptions weren't likely to break the flow.

"Were there other changes this year?"

"Some new people, but nobody else got bumped."

Unless you count Borowski and Petris, he thought.

"You'll be needing two principal players now, won't you?" he asked.

"She'll find them."

"You don't think she'll promote the second flute and oboe?"

"I'm done guessing. I wouldn't put it past her to bring in Eskimos. Might as well call it the Drop-In Symphony as the Oliver, for all it means."

"You sit behind the oboes, is that right?"

"If I bother to sit anywhere again." She was having a high old time. He wondered how many people she'd unloaded this on.

"Did you see anything out of the ordinary last Wednesday night?"

"I saw a man sicken to die. Is that what you mean?"

"Starting before that."

"Can't think of a thing."

"Did Wanda Borowski mention anything to you after she packed up the oboe?"

"Not a word."

"Tell me how it was."

Ethel's description of the rehearsal differed from the others he had heard only in the angle from which she had viewed it. She had passed up the punch table to slip outdoors for a quick cigarette during the break.

"I can tell you who all was out there, if you want to know."

"I'll keep that in mind. For the moment, I'm more interested in those of you who sat near Petris and Mrs. Borowski. Tell me, did you by chance see her on Saturday?"

"Didn't see anybody. Too busy."

"Busy?"

"Puttin' up applesauce. Twenty-eight quarts. I about melted, it was so hot."

"All by yourself?"

"Do I look as if I couldn't?" She was not amused. "Been doin' it alone since Mother had her stroke. She used to help some before that."

"Nobody dropped in that day?"

"Folks don't, mostly. I count it a big social occasion when the mail carrier honks. He likes to do that when there's something worth making a trip down to the box for."

"Did he honk Saturday?"

"No, he just waved and went on by."

"And what time was that?"

"About noon. I was sitting out here quartering apples, to get away from the kitchen. What do you want to know all this for? I didn't make a quick run into town and kill her, if that's what you're thinking."

"You've seen the paper, then," he said.

"Yes, and the TV. I saw you were looking into what happened to old George, too. Why do you think I've let you waste my time like this? But I don't see why you're so interested in who sits where."

"You may be right," he said. "It may be pure coincidence that two people who sat next to each other in the orchestra died so close together, but we'd still like to ask you to be extra careful! for a while."

"She was murdered in her own bedroom, wasn't she?" Ethel looked him straight in the eye.

"Yes."

"What do you suggest I do, quit sleeping?" She nodded triumphantly. "Just how hard do you expect it would be to get into this house? Back when it was built, the only lock anyone around here ever used was a shotgun—and I don't hold with that. Too easy to use against you. Besides, it seems to me that the people who ought to be careful are the ones who saw George drink that poison, and I wasn't there. For all I know, Wanda was right next to him then, too. Maybe you can get the word out to the murderer that I don't know a thing."

Was she laughing at him? He couldn't tell, but he took it seriously.

"I'll try. In the meantime, you'd be wise to talk that way yourself. Tell it around that you've already given the police everything you know and that they say you had no new evidence."

"I never see anyone to tell. Think I should hang a note out for the mailman?" Again, he saw that triumphant gleam in her eye.

"You might just mention it at orchestra next week."

She hmphed.

By the time he left, she was midway around the yard again. He reflected that a conductor's lot might at times be unhappier than a policeman's. Imagine having to bust Ethel Cykler down to second bassoon.

He made a mental note to check with her mailman and to talk to Bob Peterson at the *Courier* about "protection" for Ethel—and the others, for that matter. He couldn't name names; that might endanger players not mentioned. It would have to be an innocuous little statement in the context that no evidence had turned up to convince the police that Petris had been murdered. No, that was too strong—murder hadn't been mentioned there yet. He'd work it out with Bob.

He mulled over what Ethel had said. Only Wanda's murder was making him think of the circle of people around George Petris as more likely suspects—or potential victims—than anyone else in the orchestra. Long experience had taught him to distrust coincidence, but it *could* have been only coincidence. Captain Altschuler might be right that these were two entirely separate cases, united only by proximity. Ethel's idea that Wanda was standing next to George when he picked up his drink seemed more probable, he thought, and with luck he could even check it.

And then there was the oboe, or rather, there wasn't. The disappearing oboe connected the two deaths without question. But who would kill to get it? Not Daniel—all he'd have to do was ask for it. Might Wanda have noticed something about the oboe, rather than something during the rehearsal? And blurted it out to Daniel, who then silenced her with the reed knife and got rid of the oboe before calling the police? Or maybe she figured out something unrelated to the oboe, something about Daniel and his father, and he used the reed knife and got rid of it and the oboe along with it.

If Daniel had told the simple truth, though, someone else had wanted that oboe badly enough to kill for it. Not for money— not with cash and silver left behind. Sentiment seemed unlikely, too, unless Lisa Wallston was a more talented liar than he thought or the former Mrs. Petris was playing jet-set tricks. Even as he rejected the notion that she had made a flying trip to Oliver, unnoticed by anyone, he pulled over to the side of the road and wrote himself a cryptic message in the little notebook with which he clung to sanity and details: "Chk wife CA." Ketcham could handle that one. He never would have been able to explain it to Pruitt.

A woman—he tried to remember whether they'd asked the neighbors about a woman. On Saturday, he was sure, they'd all referred to the killer as "he." Had that influenced what people had told them?

Coming into town from the north, he was only a few blocks from the Borowski house. On sudden impulse, he turned onto Posey Avenue and again at Grove Street. He found a parking place a block beyond the little house. The once immaculate lawn, now badly trampled, would soon need mowing. The plants hanging over the porch were already drooping for lack of water.

He didn't expect to find as many people home at midday on a Monday as there had been on Saturday, but odds were with the old ladies next door. He twisted their old-fashioned mechanical doorbell and heard its metallic bring.

Miss Luca, the plump one, came to the door. Oh, my, yes, she'd be glad to help in any way she could. It was such an awful thing. She and Miss Hobbs had hardly slept a wink since last Saturday. You never knew when he'd come back, did you?

No, Miss Hobbs wasn't home. She'd gone over to the Senior Citizens' Center for the afternoon, hadn't left but five minutes ago. She was a great bridge player, but Miss Luca had never cared for it, herself. It seemed to change people's whole personalities. Why, he'd never believe what Miss Hobbs had said to her the last time she'd agreed to play. They'd made their bid—a person would think that would be enough. Well, of course, she always bid on the conservative side, just in case. And she was right. If she'd bid the grand slam Miss Hobbs said was in their hands that day and then forgotten to count trump as she had, it would have been simply terrible.

Well, yes, Saturday had been terrible, too, though in a different way, of course. No, she didn't remember seeing anyone near dear Wanda's house before they went in for "Masterpiece Theatre," she'd told him that before, hadn't she? But she was keeping her eyes peeled now for any suspicious-looking man, he could be sure.

A woman? Oh, no, surely not. She couldn't bear to think it. Women didn't do such terrible things. They were too sensitive and gentle. Why, just last year, when their sweet kitty had died and the mice had begun running through the kitchen just as bold as you please, she herself had scarcely been able to see to bait the trap, and when it had snapped, she'd thrown away mouse, trap, and all, because she was too softhearted to touch that furry little body.

Well, yes, she supposed there might have been a woman around when they went in, but for gracious sake, she and Miss Hobbs were there, too, and they were women.

No, she didn't remember seeing other mothers and children, but of course that didn't mean there hadn't been any. She kept a good watch on the street, he could be sure, but hardly for women and children. Well, dear Wanda was an exception. Such a considerate neighbor and such dear little children. It was so very unfortunate that that man had come at the one time in the week when she and Miss Hobbs were too busy to see what was happening.

# Chapter Twenty-Two

Miss Hobbs was busy again. Standing behind her, Fred could see no point in announcing himself until she finished finessing the queen of hearts. She was on her way to another slam, and very much in control of this one. Would she feel the need to play it out? Apparently not.

"I think the rest are ours," she said quietly, fanning her cards expertly. If he hadn't seen it, Fred wouldn't have believed her gnarled, arthritic hands capable of such dexterity.

"Well, I never," marveled her partner, whose slender fingers were covered with rings.

"Berta, I wish I knew how you did it," said the man to her right.

Miss Hobbs lowered her eyes. Fred spoke before modesty could yield to the desire for a postmortem.

"Miss Hobbs, I wonder if you'd spare me a few minutes."

She turned slowly and leaned on the table to look up at him, her spine and bent neck rigid.

"Yes, of course, Lieutenant," she said. "Muriel, will you excuse me, please? I won't be offended if you want to find another fourth."

The woman with the rings shook her head emphatically. "Not on your life," she said. "Partners like you don't grow on trees, you know. You'll wait, won't you?" she asked the others. They murmured assent and, with what Fred thought remarkable delicacy, took the cards to another table and started a game of gin rummy.

"They know how much trouble it would be to get me up and moved," Miss Hobbs said matter-of-factly, as if she'd read his mind. "Have you found out who killed my neighbor?"

"We're working on it." He took the chair vacated by the lone male bridge player. "We think we've narrowed it down a little, and I'd appreciate your help."

"I only wish I could help. It makes me so *angry*."

He knew just how she felt. But he went on.

"Maybe you can. Think back to Saturday morning. Try to see the street in your mind, as you saw it just before you went into the house. Was anybody, anybody at all, out there besides you and Mrs. Borowski?"

"The children, of course, and Miss Luca." She wasn't being flip, but seemed to be taking his question literally. Good.

"Yes. Anybody else?"

"The paper boy was already gone, no one delivers milk anymore, and the mail didn't come until after…"

"After the police arrived?"

"Yes."

"You're doing fine."

She shut her eyes, and for a moment he thought she'd fallen asleep, as his grandmother used to do, bolt upright. Little movements under the closed lids suggested, though, that she was scanning the street in her mind's eye.

"Down at the end of the block," she said, opening her eyes again, "there were some other children coming towards the park. Bigger children—maybe ten or twelve years old."

"Would you know them again if you saw them?"

"No, they were too far away. I'm not even sure if they were boys or girls. I remember they were pretty rambunctious, and one of them was bouncing a basketball."

No bouncy children had disturbed the perfect order of the Borowski living room. Scratch children.

"How about women?" he asked.

"I don't remember. Usually I don't notice people all that much, but the children reminded me of myself when I could still get around. Would you believe I played basketball? Out by the barn with my brothers, and I loved every minute of it. Something in me snaps to attention when a basketball goes by. There's nothing like that sound on a sidewalk." Her voice sounded dreamy. He didn't want to lose her.

"So you noticed the kids."

"Yes, and I'm afraid that's all I noticed. I don't remember any men or women, but that doesn't mean they weren't there. Now if you asked me about cars, it would be different."

"Cars?"

"It's a little game I play. I'm a car watcher, the way some people are birdwatchers. Miss Luca, with whom I live, was ecstatic one day last week when she saw two hummingbirds and a rufus-sided towhee in the same morning. I wouldn't hurt her feelings for the world, but I think a Porsche, an MG, and an Edsel top that any day, and I saw all three last Friday."

"Were you watching cars Saturday, too?"

"Not intentionally. It's an automatic thing, you know. Of course I know all the regulars in the neighborhood and I don't even notice them, but let a stranger drive by, and my antennae are out."

"And?"

"It was a disappointing morning. All domestic."

A wild thought occurred to Fred.

"You don't keep a tally, do you?"

"On paper? No, but I think you'll find my memory is excellent."

"Yes, ma'am, I'm sure it is." And he was. "Suppose you tell me all the vehicles you remember seeing on the street when you left Mrs. Borowski on her porch."

"A Buick Skylark, red, this year's model, with a CB antenna. Then a red Ford pickup. I'm not sure of the model year, but it was rusted out all around the fenders."

"That's it?" His pencil paused over the little notebook.

"It was quiet then. It picked up later."

"There was quite a crowd, yes."

"No, I mean while we were still watching television. Not even 'Masterpiece Theatre' can make me miss a Corvette. It was vintage 1959, in wonderful condition. Then a light blue Seville not more than a year old. After a while an elderly green Rabbit with a bad cough and a pink Pinto I hadn't seen for months. It used to go by all the time. That's all."

"Did anybody stop and park?"

"No, but they couldn't very well. There's no parking in our block."

"What about drivers, or passengers?" It was too much to ask, he was sure.

"I couldn't see them from inside the house. Besides, I told you, I watch cars, not people. My friends think I'm a little batty. Maybe they're right." From her impish grin, he could tell that her friends' opinions didn't worry her.

"Today I'd give a lot to be a people watcher instead—but it wouldn't bring her back, would it?" Now she was sober.

"No, it wouldn't." And that was the hell of it, he thought. The best you could hope for was to lay blame at the right door and put the killer out of circulation. He had no idea whether this one would kill again, anyway. He was afraid he'd find out all too soon. His own puny warnings would be forgotten as soon as the fuss died down, as it surely would without news of an arrest.

A light touch on his shoulder jolted him out of his thoughts.

"Hello, Fred. Have you come to learn bridge from the expert?" Joan stood beside Miss Hobbs, her warm eyes smiling at him.

"Not me," he said, feeling too low to think of a clever reply. "I only came to ask her another question or two."

Joan looked puzzled.

"About our neighbor, Joan," said Miss Hobbs. "She was killed on Saturday. Such a shame."

"Oh," said Joan, the light dawning. "You're—" and he saw her get stuck.

"The old biddy next door, I imagine," said Bertha Hobbs, the imp shining through her thick spectacles.

"Not quite that bad," Joan said, laughing. "Don't let me interrupt."

"I'm afraid I've told him everything I know. It's mighty little."

"Thank you, Miss Hobbs. You never know what will make a difference." Fred turned to go.

"Fred, can we talk a minute?" Joan asked.

"Oh, sure." Hearing the lack of enthusiasm in his own voice, he wondered how she would interpret it.

She led him to her cubicle.

"You look a little tired."

"I'll survive. It's not one of my better days." He sank down onto the wooden chair, wishing that it leaned back.

"I take it you didn't get my note," Joan said.

"What note?"

"Just to call." She twiddled a pencil on her desk. "I had an inspiration earlier. It's probably silly, but for a while there, I was so sure."

"A little inspiration wouldn't hurt."

"Fred, I don't think we know when Wanda died, after all."

"Oh?"

"All we know is when she was last seen and when somebody started the washer. I don't know why I didn't see it right away—listen to me, now I'm sure all over again—but that somebody wasn't Wanda."

He bit off the sarcastic remark before it reached his lips. "Go on."

"Think about it for a minute. She had her house clean, her ironing sprinkled, her supper cooking, and her kids in the park by ten-thirty in the morning—on a Saturday. You can't tell me that a woman that well organized would wash one towel and one bathrobe in that big machine and leave a laundry hamper full of dirty sheets and towels." Her eyes sparkled as she warmed to her argument. "Even if she had wanted to wash those things separately, which doesn't make sense, she'd never have left the water level at extra high."

It had a certain logic.

"But if she didn't, then—"

"Then maybe the murderer did," Joan finished triumphantly. "To clean up the blood. It would come right out in cold water if it hadn't had time to set, and since we know she was still alive twenty minutes before someone started the washer, it would hardly have set."

"I don't think the lab would even be able to identify human blood, much less type it, after that," he agreed. "But why bother washing it at all?"

"To slow you down, maybe," she suggested. "Especially if the killer knew Daniel was coming or was afraid the children were on their way home. Weren't you looking for someone covered with blood? Isn't that why you wanted to go with me to Yoichi's, because you heard about his sweaters?"

Of course it was. Even Yoichi had spotted it.

"This does change things," Fred said. "One of the reasons I couldn't see Daniel as a serious possibility was that he was completely clean. He even rolled his sleeves down to let us look. Volunteered it himself. Not that they might not have been rolled up all along, of course. I did figure our man would have blood on him somewhere. I suppose those things were hanging in the bathroom—we can ask the husband."

"Covering up with whatever was hanging in the bathroom doesn't sound like planning ahead," Joan said.

"Oh, I don't know," Fred said. He tilted the chair against the wall, finding something like his customary angle for thinking. "I suppose you would count on finding towels in any bathroom. The robe might have been a lucky break. But I think you're right about the washer. A real planner would have dumped in some other stuff, too. Sure doesn't sound much like a woman."

"Fred Lundquist, you should know better than that," Joan said, exasperation in her voice.

"Than what?"

"All women aren't like Wanda, and you know it. I'm too stingy to waste all that water, even if I'm not the perfect housewife, but I can think of lots of women who wouldn't give it a thought. Evelyn, for instance."

Evelyn Wade, of the powder blue carpets and Cadillac. Was it the light blue Seville Bertha Hobbs had spotted? He whipped out the notebook and wrote, "Chk Cad model."

Joan looked horrified. "You're not taking that down!"

"No," he said, not altogether truthfully. "It made me think of something Miss Hobbs told me." Evelyn Wade had been in all the right places at all the right times—serving drinks, picking up a babysitter at Werner's lab, and even driving by Borowskis' Saturday morning, if that was her car. A certain ruthlessness had always made him uncomfortable around Evelyn, but he balked at translating it into cold-blooded murder. The question, of course, was whether Evelyn would have balked.

"Why?" he asked. "Why would she want to kill those two?"

"I can't imagine," Joan answered, and he realized that he had spoken aloud. "I know she's a little pushy, but that's absurd."

A little pushy was not how Fred would have put it. "Probably," he said. "I'm willing to consider the absurd right now, though, and anything else that fits the facts."

"Okay, then, try this on for size. If a woman killed Wanda, then that might have been the woman Daniel talked to. Maybe that's why the oboe disappeared. When she answered the phone and heard him say he was coming, she knew she didn't have time to do much of anything but get away. So she put the robe and towel in the washer to throw you off the track, tossed the knife in the oboe case, and took off fast."

That would fit Lisa Wallston, he thought. The last person she'd want to see, even on the street, would be Daniel Petris. In that case, though, she'd have known her casual lie was doomed from the start. Surely she could have come up with something more convincing. Unless...He remembered how easily she had abandoned her story. Could she have lied so transparently on purpose, to draw attention to Daniel as a suspect, thus getting back at both Petris men and at the same time sounding so ignorant of the facts as to make herself an unlikely suspect?

Joan knew the gossip about Lisa and Daniel's father. Fred told her about the visit and his idea that Lisa and her mother might have committed the two murders independently.

She considered it for long moments. At last she said, "I met Lisa's mother yesterday in the OB ward. She's bitter, all right. I don't know how you tell whether a person is angry enough to kill. I just don't know."

Neither does anyone else, Fred thought glumly. They sat in silence, she shaking her head ever so slightly and twirling the pencil, and he letting his chin rest on his collarbone.

Another bitter person came to mind. Unsure how Joan would react, Fred kept silent. Finally, he left.

♮♮♮

Back at the station he found Sergeant Ketcham buried in the Borowski file.

"What do you think, Johnny?" Fred asked.

"Not much," Ketcham answered, scarcely looking up. "Lot of loose ends. I don't see anybody backing up the neighbors." He peered over wire-rimmed reading glasses. "Any chance they're lying?"

That was a new thought. It tasted wrong, though.

"I can't think why. They sure as hell didn't do it themselves. Miss Hobbs has all she can do to get around, and Miss Luca...well, you look for yourself. There's no reason it couldn't have been a woman, though. That reminds me, I'd like you to find out what you can about where the ex-Mrs. Petris spent last week."

"You want me to keep checking the orchestra people?"

"Let's wait until Wednesday night. It'll be a lot easier when they're all in one place."

A nagging ache reminded him that he hadn't eaten since breakfast. His watch said ten to three—it would have to wait. He was due in court at three to testify in a case involving a string of bicycle thefts. In this college town, ten-speed Peugeots and Fujis amounted to big business, legal or otherwise. On the way out the door he remembered his other note.

"Hey, Johnny," he called. "Who in town drives a Seville?"

"Not your style, Lieutenant," Ketcham answered with a grin. "Save your money. Take it from me, the lady's not worth it."

Think of icebergs, Fred told himself, but the relentless warmth rose to his cheeks. He glowered.

"Just joking, Lieutenant," Ketcham said hastily. "That's the top of the line. Rear end like a Rolls. Mrs. Wade has a new one. So does Dr. Henshaw's wife."

Great. Busting Ethel Cykler to second bassoon would be a picnic compared to coming up with iffy circumstantial evidence that linked Sam Wade's wife to a murder. Still nursing his wounds from the morning's explosion in Altschuler's office, Fred retreated to the comparatively safe territory of the courtroom.

# Chapter Twenty-Three

The bridge playerswere long gone, the last covered dish from the noonday carry-in had been tucked away for its absent-minded owner to retrieve, and only one of the adult day care participants was still waiting to be picked up. Sitting on the sofa, feet propped on a chair, Joan yielded to weariness.

"Where's Henry?" old Mrs. Skomp asked querulously for at least the fifteenth time in as many minutes.

"He's bringing the car around," Joan answered automatically, reaching over to pat the hand on which veins stood out like fat strands of overcooked spaghetti. "He'll be here soon."

She hoped it was true. Henry Skomp was effusively grateful for the respite the centre provided him from the constant care of his mother. He was also usually late when the time came to take her home again.

Hearing the door open, Joan stood to help the frail woman. To her surprise, the man who entered was not Henry Skomp but Elmer Rush.

"Well, hi, there," she said.

Already halfway across the floor, he scowled at her, or was it at Mrs. Skomp? Surely not, Joan thought. He didn't answer, but turning his back on them both, he suddenly began pushing chairs aside, throwing their cushions onto the floor, and slamming cupboard doors in the craft area.

Joan could hear him muttering under his breath. She stayed where she was, wondering whether to speak again. Mrs. Skomp stared into space. She didn't seem to notice.

"Did you forget something?" Joan finally asked inanely.

He whirled on her, not the man she had begun to think of as a friend, but an angry stranger.

"Did I ask you?"

"Hey, Elmer, it's me. Remember?"

Almost as soon as the storm had begun, it subsided.

"Looking for Julie's loom," he muttered, standing still in the middle of the room.

"Henry, come over here," came the voice from the sofa.

"It's not Henry, Mrs. Skomp," Joan said.

"Where's Henry?"

"He'll be here soon. Would you like me to turn on the television while you wait?"

"Don't like television." Mrs. Skomp snapped her pocketbook open and began searching its depths. "I wish he'd hurry up." With trembly fingers, she folded and refolded an unsullied white handkerchief.

"Dammit," Elmer muttered. He picked up a cushion.

"I hope you find it," Joan said, sinking back down. "I'll keep an eye out for it tomorrow. Tonight I seem to have run out of spizz."

"What's she doing here so late?" It felt like an accusation. "You should have closed up half an hour ago."

"We did, actually, but I couldn't walk off and leave Mrs. Skomp all alone, now could I?"

"Where's Henry?" This time it was Elmer who asked. Mrs. Skomp folded the handkerchief again.

"On his way, I hope. This is the third time he's been late like this since I've worked here. He always shows up eventually. It's hard on his mother, though. She manages all right during the day, but she'd been ready to go home since the first person left at four, and here we still are at five-thirty, with nothing to hold her interest."

Elmer exploded.

"Irresponsible, that's what it is! I'd like to teach him a thing or two!"

His color was rising as high as his voice and he jabbed his finger at her. Joan tried to calm him down.

"Elmer, I'm sure there's some good reason for his being late."

"Then he should have called. He's using you and abusing her, that's what he's doing. I won't have it! I'll take her home myself." He started toward the sofa, his face a thundercloud. In the cocoon of her own world, Mrs. Skomp didn't respond.

"Elmer, he wouldn't know where she was." Neither would Mrs. Skomp, but an inner voice told Joan not to say it.

"Give him a taste of his own medicine! He ought to realize that losing your marbles doesn't mean losing your feelings, too!"

Something clicked.

"Elmer, has someone been hurting Julie's feelings?" Joan asked.

He looked startled.

"How did you—?"

"Where's Henry?" asked Mrs. Skomp.

"Here I am, Mother," he said coming in the door with a jaunty step. "Sorry I'm so late. One last customer was in the store and I didn't have the heart to shoo her out when we locked the door. She was buying a gift for her first great-grandchild."

Joan shot a quick look at Elmer. He was still frowning.

Henry's smile was disarming.

"I'm grateful to you both for waiting with her. I don't know what we'd do without this program. It came along just in time to spare her a nursing home. I'd hate that. She's all I have."

"We're glad to have her, Mr. Skomp," Joan said carefully. "But if you really need someone here past five, and I think you do, we should arrange it formally instead of leaving your mother here after hours day after day. It's hard on her and hard on the staff." Meaning me, she thought. "I'd be happy to arrange an extra half hour with one of the regular day care program people. There might even be others who could use the service."

"That would be grand," he said, flashing that smile again. "And of course I'd want to pay for the extra time. It's well worth it to know that she's happy. Please, let me at least drive you home."

That should make Elmer feel better, Joan thought, but when she turned again to look, he was gone.

"Thanks, but I think I'd rather walk tonight," she told Henry Skomp.

The walk home revived her. She could smell the promise of frost in the cool evening air. Counting back, she remembered seeing her first firefly more than three months ago—frost was overdue. But that hadn't been in Oliver. She supposed it didn't count.

Andrew was hard at work, books and papers spread all over the kitchen table. He'd already made himself a sandwich and was holding it in one hand while scribbling notes with the other.

"D'you mind eating in the living room?" he asked. "Three tests tomorrow."

"Sure. What do you want?"

"Nothing." He looked down at the sandwich and said sheepishly, "Well, nothing fancy. I'll just take care of myself, okay?"

"Okay." Far be it from me to get in your way, she thought. What a familiar refrain that was at the center, at least among those who had all their marbles, as Elmer put it. She thought of the others, the Mrs. Skomps. Which would be worse, to be afraid to visit the children you loved for fear of intruding on their lives, or to be so lost that you couldn't control what you did, or what they did to you?

For all Henry Skomp's sweet words, she wondered how his mother fared at home. Was he as casual about her needs there as he was about letting her wait at the center? Still, she seemed hardly to know where she was much of the time. Wouldn't it be even harder to be overworked and overworried at that age, as Elmer was?

Joan ate her own sandwich thoughtfully. In the corner, the box of music reminded her mutely of things left undone. Well, it would have to wait. She'd practice Tuesday night, after Andrew's tests. On the other hand, she supposed marking the parts for Yoichi was unlikely to disturb his studying.

She sharpened a number 2 pencil with the butcher knife and set to it, copying the little vees and staple shapes that would tell all the violas to bow up or down at the same time. She was delighted to see that the orchestra had ordered an extra part. It meant a little more copying, but it also meant that she could probably keep one to practice most of the time. Making quick work of the violas, she reached for the second violin parts still in the box.

Then she saw the familiar prescription bottle that had been hidden beneath them and all at once she knew.

She knew how George had died.

She knew why Wanda had been murdered.

She knew who was now in greatest danger.

Choking back the impulse to tell Andrew, she reached with amazingly steady fingers for the telephone.

# Chapter Twenty-Four

Joan scrubbed at her fingertips, feeling like Lady Macbeth. Now on cardboard, her spots would be compared to those on the prescription bottle labeled with the name of George Petris, but she couldn't wash away her guilt or her fear.

Fred had met her at the police station. She watched him seal and initial the plastic evidence bag. He laid her print card in a drawer marked To Be Classified, pulled up a swivel chair for her, and tilted his own back at an alarming angle.

"We'll test for latents in the morning," he said. "There's not a chance in a thousand we'll find anything usable, but we'll never know until we eliminate your prints. I don't know how tricky it is to detect that poison, either." He sounded bored by the prospect of sifting through the new evidence.

An inarticulate sound of misery began in Joan's throat. She was beginning to shake. He leaned forward and touched her hand.

"Joan, are you all right?" he asked, his voice a little more human.

"No, I'm not all right!" she snapped. "I'm scared, and I keep thinking that if I'd seen the reeds Thursday or Friday, Wanda would still be alive. It's all my fault, and next time it could be me."

She heard the wild note in her own voice. I'm not going to be hysterical, she told herself. I'm in control. She shut her eyes, inhaling one long, slow breath and letting it out just as slowly.

"How do you figure that?" Fred asked quietly. She opened her eyes and saw support in his.

"Once we were looking for a way George could have been poisoned, I should have thought of the reeds right away. Oboe players spend half their lives sucking reeds unless they bring water to rehearsal, especially the way Alex rehearses this orchestra. We didn't have an A from the oboe to tune by the second half, but George had a solo after the first few bars of music. He was sitting there sucking on a reed, all ready to play, when Alex stopped us strings to work over the pom-poms."

"The what?"

She found a faint grin somewhere. Good, she thought. I must be calming down.

"We keep the beat, pom-pom-pom-pom, pom-pom-pom-pom, and the cellos do a little dum-de-dum-de-duh-um, dum-de-dum-de-dum before the oboe comes with duh-um, de-dum-de-dum-de-duh-ump, dum-dum-duh-um-duh-um." She sang the little tune from the second movement of the Schubert, beating pom-poms against his desk with her hand.

"You'll do Bernstein out of a job." Fred was smiling now.

"Funny man. Anyway, George didn't even make it that far after he sat there with the reed in his mouth while we ran through the pom-poms."

"Nobody could count on that but the conductor."

"No, but it's a long solo and the oboe plays all through the movement. It would have gotten to him sooner or later."

"Anyone would know that?" he asked without enthusiasm.

"Yes. We played through it the week before. The overture has a big oboe solo, too, for that matter."

"What about the first half? Did he play then?"

"Yes. We read through the last movement first. He had a fat part and he sounded fine. We sat out while Alex worked over a bad spot with the violins and then we all took a break."

"So whether it was the reeds or the Kool-Aid, the poison was administered during the intermission."

His matter-of-fact tone was helping, but Joan was sure.

"You know it was the reeds. If I'd found them sooner, the killer wouldn't have gone to Wanda's looking for them and ended up killing her, too. It took a while for the word to get around that you thought George was murdered. At first they all thought he was just sick. I thought so, too. No one took Yoichi seriously. And Fred, that's why the oboe disappeared. The murderer had no way of knowing the reeds weren't in the case with the instrument."

A thought hit her. "That means at least Nancy didn't do it. She saw me pick up the bottle."

"Maybe," he said. "Maybe not." He held up the bag and peered through it at the bottle. "We don't know what happened to the reed that was on the oboe when Petris collapsed. If it was packed in the oboe case, then it wouldn't matter when you found these."

Maybe she hadn't been harboring a murder weapon in her living room after all. She wasn't comforted.

"If you could figure that out now, you'd have figured it out then, too, and gone after it in time."

"That's funny," he said slowly.

Not very, she thought, disappointed in him. He thrust the bag under her nose and tilted it.

"Look at that. Isn't that a bassoon reed?"

It was. Joan remembered Elmer's embarrassment.

"You're right," she said. "While Alex was drilling the violins, George was holding forth to Elmer on the only right way to wrap a reed. She shushed them. Elmer was so embarrassed that he stuck his reed in George's bottle." She put her hand on his arm. "Oh, Fred, I feel better. What if I'd seen that first and given the bottle to Elmer instead of you? He might have died, too."

Relief swept over her. It didn't last.

"He might have been perfectly safe," Fred said. "Suppose I wanted to poison Petris's reeds. What could be easier? I grab my chance when the conductor distracts him, lean forward, and drop my reed in his bottle. A little white powder on it and I've set the trap."

"You don't mean it." Joan shifted uneasily and hugged her elbows.

Fred leaned back so far that she thought he would surely topple over until she saw the toes hooked under his bottom drawer.

"How much do you know about Elmer Rush?" he asked finally.

"Fred, you can't imagine that sweet old man would do such a thing!"

"Have you ever seen him angry?" Fred tilted still farther back, cradling his head in his crossed hands.

"Well...once." She didn't want to consider it. There had to be a world of difference between a murderous rage and stomping around because you'd lost something. Besides, Elmer hadn't really been that angry about the lost loom. It was some slight to Julie, though he'd left before saying what it was.

"And what would you say is his chief concern?"

That was easy. "Julie. He's wonderful with her, Fred. You should see them."

"I have." Fred brought his feet down on the floor and looked her in the eye. "Tell me, what do you think would happen if he recognized George Petris as the lifeguard who nearly let Julie drown?"

"That's impossible!"

"Is it? The accident happened in California," he said. "We know Petris grew up in California. Daniel says he was a strong swimmer. If he was over eighteen, there ought to be a record."

"He wasn't, but she was," Joan said, remembering. "The babysitter he was drinking and making out with when he should have been watching Julie. Elmer said she served some time. You could find out."

It was still unthinkable. She could no more imagine Elmer poisoning George, much less cutting Wanda's throat, than she could imagine herself doing it.

"I can't believe it, Fred," she insisted. "Not Elmer."

The words echoed hollowly in her mind. Hadn't she imagined a whole town saying them about the man who had tried to force himself on her? Wouldn't she have been the first to say them about him if she had heard him accused by another?

Suddenly she could feel the letter opener in her hand again, cool and heavy. How close had she been to murder that day in the church? Close enough not to trust herself to go back, she knew. She had fled all the way to Oliver instead.

I wasn't afraid of him, she thought, even when I should have been. I was afraid of myself. How could I ever wonder what Elmer might be capable of?

"You haven't talked to him," Fred was saying.

"No."

"I don't need to tell you not to. Just remember, we're a long way from proving it. We'll give you some protection until the next rehearsal. Then you'll give the reeds to me in front of the whole orchestra."

"But I don't have them anymore."

"Only you and I know that."

"Oh." Oh.

"I'll return the bottle to you Wednesday, before the rehearsal. It will look the same, but it won't be the same. Don't worry. You'll be fine."

"And Elmer? Will he be fine?" It came bursting out of her. "Look at Julie! What George did to her was murder, too, in a way. But the law couldn't touch him. Is it so terrible if Elmer took it upon himself?"

Immediately, guilt assailed her. Who was she to value George's life so lightly? She fought back. Who was George to value Julie's so little?

"I don't want to argue that with you," Fred said quietly. "But how do the Borowskis come into your rough justice? What's their crime?"

She had forgotten Wanda, and remembering brought back her fear. Wanda's crime had consisted of being in the way. She'd known that the minute she'd found the reeds.

"Do you...do you think he'd really kill anybody else?"

"Anybody who gets in his way." He might have been reading her mind. "Even if you think killing Petris was an execution of sorts, it was planned. He didn't just happen to have that poison in his pocket, you know. I don't think he expected to have to kill Mrs. Borowski, though. That smacked of spur-of-the-moment improvisation. Military training, too, possibly—that silent throat cutting from behind. Has Rush ever talked about the war?"

"It never came up."

"I'll do some checking." He spoke more gently. "I'm still following some other leads, Joan. I won't forget them. But be careful. If I'm right about Rush, that sweet old man gulled Wanda Borowski into letting him into her very bedroom before he killed her. My guess is that he asked to see the oboe."

"A bassoon player might want one." Joan was trying to think rationally. "Some double reed players do play all three—oboe, English horn, and bassoon. She'd believe him if he said he was interested in buying it. He could say he'd talked to Daniel and was picking it up to try it out. After all, it wasn't Wanda's to sell. But he wouldn't know that Daniel had just called her to say he was on his way to pick it up himself. She probably blurted it out."

"Maybe even challenged his story. Could be."

"So he killed her to keep her from telling."

"And to give himself a chance to dispose of the evidence. Only by now he knows he didn't get it all."

Joan looked at the reeds again and shuddered.

She was home and in bed before it hit her that the biggest mouth in town knew who had really taken them home.

# Chapter Twenty-Five

Fred Lundquist buttered his third slice of toast and opened Tuesday morning's *Courier* to Peterson's latest story.

No longer front page news, the Borowski murder investigation rated only a few column inches and an 18-point headline. Bob had done a convincing job of portraying the police as stymied for lack of evidence. He quoted Ethel Cykler directly. Her remarks cut through his vague intimations of a phantom with a grudge against wind players.

"'You ask me, I'll tell you. I think George Petris just up and died. It beats me how you could think a sick man has anything to do with a woman who gets her throat cut in her own bedroom. The police ought to quit asking silly questions and find that maniac before he kills somebody else,' Ms. Cykler told this reporter," the article ran.

Fred winced. That should take care of Ethel, he thought, but it added one more stone to the load he felt dragging him down. Altschuler would probably chew him out again, and he didn't think explaining was likely to improve matters. He lavished strawberry jam on his toast, but he might have been eating sand.

A few days earlier he would have been crowing about the evidence he expected to find in the reed bottle Joan had brought in. Today he doubted his ability to find it, and his own speculation about Elmer Rush was beginning to seem as far-fetched to him as it had to her. Yet she had stood up to the possibility, distasteful though it obviously was to her. Hadn't seemed to hold it against him, either. So why wasn't he eager to follow through?

The heaviness in his chest told him it was because he didn't want to face Altschuler and Wade. Snap out of it, Lundquist, he preached. There's nothing new about this, except this time they said it to your face instead of behind your back. You haven't changed.

But he knew he had. The night before, he had scarcely been listening to Joan, even as he had automatically pieced together a case against Rush that had finally convinced her. He'd ordered a patrol for her house and then put the whole thing out of his mind and settled down to watch the Cubs lose one last game to Cincinnati. He no longer cared. Only the belief that the murderer might kill again was making him even go through the motions.

♮♮♮

No one penetrated his gloom with so much as a greeting when he dragged into work late. Ketcham, shrewder than he was generally credited with being, stood silently drinking coffee. Fred flipped through his little notebook, deciding what to delegate.

"You remember I asked you the other day about a Seville," he said finally.

Ketcham gulped the last of his coffee and crumpled the cup. "Yeah."

"Just for kicks, go down the orchestra personnel list and see how many other matches you can make with these cars." He tore a page out of the notebook. "A '59 Corvette, a green Rabbit— probably at least five years old, a pink Pinto, a new red Skylark, and an old Ford pickup, also red. Start with the people and give me anything close."

"Okay. Anything else?"

"I'll let you know."

Ketcham disappeared with the list, not pushing for more than Fred wanted to tell.

The pathologist didn't answer his call, but Professor Werner invited him to bring his sample over to the lab to test it for TTX.

"I'm preparing a frog this morning anyway. If your stuff acts like my stuff, that ought to be pretty good confirmation. We can document it with photographs. Got a Polaroid?"

"I'll bring one."

The phone rang as soon as he put the receiver down. He was startled to hear Catherine's voice. Listening to her musical laugh, he wondered how it had held him and realized with some satisfaction that he had not once thought of her since she had last hung up on him. Otherwise occupied, he had managed to forget to apologize again for the sourdough debacle. It didn't matter.

"You poor dear." She had gone from furious to coy without benefit of flowers. "I read all about it. I understand completely. I want you to let me fix you a perfectly scrumptious lunch today— I know you never eat right when you're on a big case. I just won't take no for an answer. About eleven?"

"Sure, Catherine," he said. "Why not? Thanks."

"Bye, now." Her laugh tinkled in his ear again.

Where does she get that "big case" nonsense? he wondered. Only reason I have this one is that nobody else expected it to be anything but a nuisance. It had indeed been a nuisance to Catherine. The least he could do was show up and act civil.

An hour later, he was standing over Professor Werner in the lab, looking down at a frog blanketed by a wet paper towel. In his pocket Fred fingered the test tube into which he had decanted less than a teaspoonful of the water from the reed bottle. Much of the intervening time had been taken up with forms—to check out the Polaroid, to requisition film for it, even to requisition the test tube. The only thing he hadn't had to fill out in triplicate was a request for the water. He shook his head at the wonderful bureaucracy that was more concerned about pilfered test tubes than about preserving the chain of evidence. At the last minute, his innate caution had prompted him to do it right. He had interrupted Ketcham's search to have him witness the transfer of fluid and had asked him to come take notes at the lab.

The three men were cramped inside a small metal mesh enclosure. Werner explained that it screened out electrical interference from lights, motors, and recording equipment.

"The electrical signals I'm measuring here are so weak that they're covered up by anything from outside. Now let's see...I guess for your purpose, we can use plain air as a stimulant. All you want to know is the difference between how the frog responds to a puff of air before we give it some of your sample and how it responds afterwards. So, I'll aim a little puff right now. Keep your eye on the oscilloscope. It's a nice machine. I got it surplus from Purdue when they bought a fancy new model."

A wobbly line on the screen exploded into spikes and valleys, and then tapered back to what it had been.

"That's the response you get to air before you administer the TTX," Werner said. "Got your camera? We'll do it again."

Laying the print on a shelf to dry, proof that the frog had been free of tetrodotoxin when they arrived, Fred handed over the test tube.

"Will this be enough?"

"If it's any concentration at all, a drop is more than we need."

With a syringe that looked like a fever thermometer, the plunger a thin wire through the middle and the needle almost invisible, Werner injected a tiny amount of the liquid into the exposed brain tissue.

"I'm probably fussier about this than I need to be, but I always try to keep the TTX away from the afferent nerves. I want it to affect only the post-synaptic neurons, the voltage-dependent sodium channels."

Ketcham's pen had been moving steadily. Now it stopped.

"Could you spell a couple of those for me, sir?" he asked.

"Sorry," Werner said. "You don't want all that. Just write that I put some of your sample in the frog's olfactory bulb. O L and factory. One word."

The effect was rapid. By the third puff of air, five minutes after the first, the dramatic spikes on the oscilloscope had flattened out. The wobbly line rose smoothly and fell again, drawing a single gentle hill on the screen.

Werner's shoulders dropped.

"Damn," he said quietly.

"Sir?" said Ketcham.

"I'd been hoping...well, never mind. What's done is done. The stuff you have there is almost certainly from my lab."

"Couldn't anything else do that?" Fred asked.

"Not really, not in that tiny amount. I don't suppose you'll tell me where you found it."

"Not just now," Fred said.

"Figured as much. Well, let's get the picture. I'll give you some prints of results I got with TTX. You'll see that they're identical to these. You'll be able to confirm it chemically. The chemical structure of TTX is unique."

The clock in the ivy-covered bell tower struck eleven as Ketcham and Lundquist left the biology building. They walked in silence to Fred's Chevy.

"You drive, Johnny," he said, handing over the keys and climbing into the passenger seat. "Drop me at Catherine's, will you? I'll walk back after lunch."

$\oint\oint\oint$

Catherine didn't look like a woman who had spent the morning slaving over a hot stove. Only her fiery hair looked anything but cool and crisp, and she had contained it sleekly with a ribbon. She had, however, gone all out. Although he had never figured out what she put into the savory dish she served him, Fred recognized its creamy sauce and resolved to do it justice. Crisp green salad with fresh herb dressing complemented the rich casserole. She hadn't wasted on him the frilly touches that made Oliver hostesses compete for her decorative platters, but the fruit bowl, he knew, had been arranged as much by color as by taste. He began to relax.

"Like it?" she asked.

"You know I do. You're a terrific cook, Catherine."

"As good as that Mrs. Spencer?" She smirked at him. "I hear you've been sampling her goodies."

With difficulty, Fred resisted the almost overwhelming temptation to hit her or stalk out. He should have known what was coming.

"Catherine, don't get started." He could feel the cream curdling in his stomach.

"Get started? What do you mean?" Her voice dripped honey. "Surely it's no secret that you've been seeing her, or is it? I heard you were turning into bosom buddies. I'd like to know where that leaves me."

Fred put down his fork.

"Since you brought it up, that leaves you sounding like a woman who wants to run my life. Maybe this is news to you, Catherine. I plan to run my own life and choose my own friends.

I won't dance for a jealous woman who wants to pull puppet strings. I don't know many men who would."

"Don't you? No wonder you can't solve that murder." Her eyes glinted.

Fred stood up, abandoning dinner entirely.

"What do you mean?" he demanded.

For a moment, he thought she was going to engage in a childish game of "Wouldn't you like to know?" Whether she was intimidated or couldn't resist the gossip, he couldn't tell, but she answered him.

"For goodness sake, Fred, I'm only saying what everyone knows, and you would, too, if you understood anything about people at all."

"Catherine..." He stared her down.

"Oh, all right," she said. "Hasn't it ever occurred to you that Sam Wade jumps every time Evelyn pulls a string, as you put it? I can't see what he sees in her, but she's had him hook, line, and sinker ever since they were kids. Of course, a good-looking man like that is always going to have—shall we call them admirers? And he's no saint, but Evelyn knows just how far to let his line run out before she reels him in again. She expects big things of him. The White House, some say. I wouldn't put it past her to get rid of anybody Sam took a serious interest in. You'd hardly expect him to look sideways at that boring little Mrs. Borowski, but you never know. Still waters run deep."

Mighty deep, Fred thought. Not a word of this particular scandal had reached him, for all the calls he'd had about the philandering George Petris. Not that it couldn't be true.

"Catherine, are you seriously suggesting that Sam Wade was having an affair with Wanda Borowski and that Evelyn got jealous and killed her?"

"I didn't say she was jealous. I'd be surprised if she cared whose bed he parks his shoes under, but if she thought he was about to wreck his political future by messing around with a married woman too close to home, she just might. She's put too much time and energy into Sam to let him get away now."

Like an investment, Fred thought. Evelyn would not be one to cut her losses. Was that what Catherine was doing? Or didn't she realize what she was revealing of herself?

He opened his mouth to contradict her, remembered the blue Seville, and shut it again.

"Fred, your dinner's getting cold," Catherine reproached him.

"I'm sorry, Catherine. I have to leave," he blurted, and did.

♮♮♮

He was glad to be on foot. Behind a wheel, he probably would have run down the first poor slob who looked at him crooked. Gradually, his jerky, angry strides began to fall into a rhythm that eased his tension. He swung along with no particular goal in mind except to get away from Catherine.

By the time he heard the college chimes strike noon, he felt ready to face another human being, if not yet Altschuler and Wade. He took a chance on finding Martha Lambert at home alone.

She came to the door smiling and wiping her hands on a dish towel.

"Why, hello, Lieutenant," she said. "Won't you come in? You just missed my father. He took Julie out for the afternoon."

She held the door for him and swiped at the dog hairs on the sofa with the towel.

"That's fine," he said, sitting down. "This time I came to see you. Are you all right?"

"Yes, thank you." She sat on the arm of the sofa. "I feel a little silly about the other day. It was one of his bad days. They don't happen often, but when they do, I lose all perspective. I'm sorry I bothered you."

"It was no bother. That's what we're here for. You kept that phone number I gave you, I hope."

Her hand flashed to her bosom.

"Yes."

Good.

"I have just a couple of questions."

"Anything, if it will help you."

♮♮♮

When he left her, he headed directly for the hospital. Negotiating with practiced ease the maze of temporary corridors born of new construction, he found the pathologist in his laboratory.

"Good to see you, Fred," Dr. Henshaw said, stripping a pair of thin rubber gloves from his fingers and tossing them into a plastic-lined wastebasket. "I was going to send some results over to you, but this makes it easier."

"Actually, I came to ask whether you'd tested the exhibits I sent you the other day for blood."

"Funny, that's just what I was going to tell you. Is that the message you left this morning?"

"No, that's another story entirely. We seem to have found the poison that did in George Petris. Professor Werner provided pretty conclusive evidence that it's the TTX he uses."

"Good thing. I couldn't have done it so fast. Let me show you what we did find."

♮♮♮

The shift had changed when Fred returned to the station, whistling. So had the very air he breathed.

Kyle Pruitt, on his way out the door, grinned at him and said, "Hi ya, Lieutenant. How's it going?"

"Hello, Kyle," Fred said. "Not bad, not bad at all. Is Altschuler in?"

"Yeah, but I think he's about to take off."

"Then I'm just in time."

Fred flipped quickly through the notes on his desk. Ketcham had left one phone memo, from the San Jose police. Mrs. Petris, they said, had been housebound for more than a week with a broken leg. The police ambulance had taken her to the emergency room the previous Monday. A briefer note summarized the results of Ketcham's vehicle registration search.

Sergeant Pruitt would have been astonished to learn that the tune the lieutenant was whistling when he arrived—and when he knocked on the captain's door—was the oboe solo from the second movement of Schubert's C Major Symphony, the "Great."

# Chapter Twenty-Six

Joan dreaded Wednesday's rehearsal. She drew the line at riding with Nancy. Not wanting to explain, she talked Andrew into phoning for her after breakfast that morning. He dragged his feet.

"Why?" he asked. "What am I supposed to say?"

"You don't know why. You don't have to lie."

"Can I tell her you're coming?"

"If she asks."

He carried it off with aplomb, hung up, and turned on her.

"I thought she was your best friend."

That stung.

"I don't seem to have a best friend anymore."

"You have me." He hugged her less clumsily than usual.

"Aw," she said, hugging him back.

"Aw," he echoed, and grinned. "Gotta go, Mom. Don't wait supper tonight. I promised Mr. Werner I'd work in the lab. I'll grab something."

"Move the dirty socks off the sofa first!" But he was gone.

♭♭♭

All day she felt uneasy. By the time Henry Skomp finally arrived to pick up his mother, Joan was leery enough of walking home alone to accept the ride he offered.

Without Andrew, the little house was quiet. She was tempted to flick on the radio, but she resisted, determined to get in half an hour's practicing before supper. Reaching into the box of music folders for the one in which she had marked her fingerings, she felt again her shock at finding the bottle of reeds there. Suddenly, Elmer's behavior at the center on Monday made sense. She dropped the music and dialed Fred's number.

She barely recognized his cheery hello.

"Fred, is that you?"

"Sure is. What's up?"

"You—you said you'd give me back the reeds so I could give them to you at rehearsal."

"I'll stop by before you leave. Ten past seven okay?"

"I'd better go a little earlier, since I have all the music. And, Fred—I've figured out something about Elmer."

"Tell me when I get there." He hung up.

No longer in any mood to practice, or cook, either, she gave in to the radio after all, changed to jeans and sneakers, and made a meal of leftovers.

Fred arrived at seven in a suit and tie. He presented the reed bottle with a flourish.

"Want me to carry the music?" he offered.

"Yes. No. Please, won't you just sit down and listen for a minute?"

He sat, pulling up the crease in each trouser leg and straightening his tie.

"Yes, ma'am, I'm listening."

What had gotten into him? Joan plunged ahead.

"You remember asking me if I'd ever seen Elmer angry?"

"Mm-hmm."

"And I said I had, once. I didn't tell you it was only the other day. He came into the center when I should have been on my way home, and he was furious. I was stuck there waiting for one of our adult day care people to be picked up. I got the impression that someone had said something unkind about Julie. He jumped all over me about how people don't care. Finally, Henry Skomp came to pick up his mother and offered me a ride home. Elmer disappeared.

"But suppose he knew I had the bottle. Nancy might have mentioned it. He must have been expecting to find me there alone, or even walking home. If the Skomps hadn't been in the way, he would have offered me a ride and I probably would have accepted and invited him in. Now I have to go to that rehearsal. Fred, I don't want to go."

"But you're all right. And you will be, I promise. Trust me." His eyes crinkled at the edges. He leaned toward her. "Here's what I need for you to do tonight."

♩♩♩

The box of music pulled on Joan's right arm. Her shoulder bag bumped the hand that carried the viola. Parking at the far end of the lot from the cars huddled near the entrance had seemed the cautious thing to do, especially when she had recognized Nancy's Olds and Elmer's VW side by side. Fred's Chevy was next in line, though, she saw when she came closer.

Still puzzled, she stopped to switch hands. Her role was clear. But what could have changed the morose man she had seen Monday night to this almost offensively self-confident one?

In the auditorium, she didn't see him at first. She handed the music up to Yoichi, who began setting folders out on the stands. Then she checked her strings against the tuning fork in her case. It was much easier than tuning with trumpets noodling behind her. Hugging her shoulder bag as if it contained diamonds, she climbed to the stage and looked around.

There in place of George Petris sat Fred Lundquist, holding a curved soprano saxophone, of all things. He might have told me, she thought. No wonder he looked so smug. Wherever did he find a soprano—a curved one at that?

She wondered whether he would actually try to play. In his big hands, the little sax looked more like a meerschaum pipe than a real instrument. It could probably hit the notes—she wasn't sure how high a soprano went. He'd have to transpose, though. The oboe part would be written in concert pitch, and she knew the soprano sax was a B-flat instrument.

Gradually, the other players were taking their places. Joan thought the second flutist had moved up to first. It looked as if most people had shown up, but the usual chatter was subdued.

Yoichi, handing out the last folders to the basses and cellos, saw her coming.

"Thank you for marking the bowings," he said, with his pixie smile.

"You're welcome. Do you need me now?"

"No. We are ready."

Joan sat down beside John Hocking, who was staring openly at Fred and the sax.

"What won't they think of next?" he said. "You suppose we'll tune to a B-flat?"

"No, here comes Sam," she said.

Sam Wade raised an inquiring eyebrow at Fred.

"Evening, Sam," Fred said. "I'm playing George Petris tonight."

"Play it any way you want to," Sam said. He set a shot glass full of water and reeds on the floor, sat down, ran a feather through the pieces of his oboe, and began fitting them together. Sucking on a reed, he stood the instrument on its six-legged support while he closed the case and sorted through the music on his stand. Joan watched, fascinated.

The concertmaster, whose name Joan still hadn't learned, stood, hesitated only a moment, and then pointed his bow at Sam for the long A. Sam put the reed into the top of his oboe, blew a couple of quick runs, and held the tuning fork to his ear.

Joan checked her tuning quickly. She made one small adjustment and sat back in comfort before the first brass note barged in.

Finally, Alex Campbell mounted the podium.

"You all know what happened this week," she said simply. "We have lost two fine musicians."

Thank you, Joan thought, for not pretending.

"A Requiem Mass will be said for Wanda Borowski tomorrow at St. Paul's. You may want to contribute toward the cost of flowers from the orchestra. There will be no services for George Petris. We're contributing in his memory to the Oliver College scholarship fund." She paused. "Some people have suggested dedicating this first concert of the season to George and Wanda. If you are in favor of doing so, would you please stand?"

One by one, in silence, the entire orchestra rose. Alex waited a long moment. Then she nodded, and they took their seats again. A lump swelled in Joan's throat. The formal gesture went a long way toward erasing her bitterness about the comments she had heard after George was taken away.

"We have been asked to do one thing more," Alex said. "I think we owe it to George. Detective Lieutenant Lundquist will explain what he needs. Lieutenant?"

She stepped down and Fred stood among the woodwinds.

"Thank you," he said. "You probably already know that I am in charge of investigating both these deaths. I'm at a considerable disadvantage with respect to Mr. Petris. By the time the police were called in, all of you had gone about your business and the janitor had cleaned the building. We've talked with some of you, but it would help if we could see where people were and what they were doing in the last few minutes before he was taken ill." He turned around. "Sergeant Ketcham, where are you?"

"Back here," a deep voice called from behind the basses. Looking back, Joan was surprised to see Evelyn Wade and Glenda Wallston standing at the refreshment table. Their bowl and platter were empty, but they had set out cups and stood ready to serve imaginary punch and cookies. Beside them, a middle-aged man in a dark suit and wire-rimmed glasses held a notebook and pencil.

"What if I don't want to?" asked one of the young second violinists. His voice shook.

"You don't have to," Fred answered. "This is entirely voluntary. If you aren't planning to participate, I'd appreciate it if you'd sit back in the audience for a few minutes. Unless..." He looked to the conductor.

"That should work," Alex said. "Go behind the rows where people leave their cases, Tad. No one spends the intermission back there."

"It's all right," the boy muttered. "I guess I'll do it."

"Come to think of it, you'd better all know your rights," Fred said. "Read 'em the Miranda, would you, Johnny?"

Sergeant Ketcham obliged, reading constitutional rights to silence and the advice of a court-appointed lawyer, all in a bored voice.

"Anyone else?" Fred asked. No one moved. "Then please do whatever you did at the beginning of the intermission last week. I'll represent George Petris. You'll need to tell me what to do."

Joan was puzzled. Why this game? But the others were already beginning to move.

"You put away your instrument and start over to the refreshments," Sam directed Fred.

"No, before that you must have put the lid on your reeds," Joan said. "I found them this way when I fell." She gave him the prescription bottle from her purse. He took it, put the sax in its case, and walked back toward the table.

Joan left John and Sam sitting, took an empty cup herself, wishing for real ice, spoke to Yoichi, and walked around the orchestra pretending to put music on the stands. Out of the corner of her eye she could see Sergeant Ketcham taking notes. Only when she came back to her seat did she again remember her headlong plunge into Sam Wade's lap. Even in blue jeans, she couldn't bring herself to repeat it intentionally.

His eyes smiled at her. He, too, had remembered.

"Sam, I can't," she said.

"Sure you can," said John Hocking. "Fake it. Knock down the stand, anyway, and whack the chairs a little."

Suddenly, it was a relief to be asked to do something destructive. With abandon, Joan lashed out at the stand, sent the music flying, and skidded Fred's chair back into Elmer's, spilling the water in which Elmer's reed was soaking. A thin stream trickled towards the pages on the floor.

"Grab the music!" Joan made a dive for it.

Fred loomed over her. "What on earth?"

"Come on, Fred, help pick it up!" She scrabbled on her hands and knees, rescuing the precious rented pages. Sam helped. Fred just watched, as did other orchestra members close enough to notice the commotion.

"You're supposed to yell at her," John commented. "That's what George did."

"Is that right?" Fred asked her. "This happened last week, too?"

"More or less. He did shout, but I got carried away tonight. Last week most of the damage I did was to my nylons. It would have been worse if Sam hadn't caught me."

"My pleasure," Sam said, with that smile that left her weak-kneed.

"And after that?" Fred pursued it.

"And after that I put everything back and about then I think we started the second half."

"Okay, let's do it." Fred spoke quietly to Alex, who called Yoichi. The players who had left the stage straggled back with relative speed.

The concertmaster rose to tune, but sat down in embarrassment when his stand partner reminded him that he had been too late the week before.

To Joan's right, Fred had opened the bottle of reeds and was offering it to Sam.

"Thanks," Sam said. "I can use them. Say, Elmer, this one's yours." He stretched to pass the bottle to Elmer.

"I wondered where that went," Elmer said, reaching forward to pick out the unfinished bassoon reed.

"Stop right there," said Fred, his long arm catching Elmer's hand before it touched the reed.

"I'll take that, if you don't mind." Sergeant Ketcham plucked the bottle from Sam's hand.

"What's going on?" a dozen voices demanded, Elmer's and Sam's among them.

Fred was on his feet.

"Gideon Samuel Wade, you're under arrest. Before I ask you any questions, I must advise you of your constitutional rights. You must understand your rights. You have the right to remain silent—"

"I know my rights, Fred," Sam interrupted. "What's all this?"

A wail came from backstage.

"You're crazy! Sam, stop him!"

Gone was Evelyn's reserve. Eyes blazing, hair flying, her dress catching on the music stands she shoved out of her way, she pushed to the front.

"Sam, say something!"

He put put out a hand toward her, palm down. "Calm down, Evelyn."

"Just a minute, please, ma'am," Fred said formally. "I have to do this right. I'm not going to get this one thrown out of court. Sam, you have the right to remain silent. Anything you say can be used against you in court."

"Sam, your career! You can't let him do this!" Evelyn cried.

"This is ridiculous," Sam began, but Fred cut him off.

"You know you'd be the first to insist on it," he said. "You have the right to talk with a lawyer for advice before I ask you any questions and to have him present during questioning. If you cannot afford a lawyer, one will be appointed to represent you during any questioning, if you wish."

"I can afford a lawyer."

"If you decide to answer questions now without a lawyer present, you will still have the right to stop answering questions at any time. You also have the right to stop answering questions at any time until you speak to a lawyer."

He turned to Ketcham.

"Did I leave anything out?"

"No, you got it all, Lieutenant," said Ketcham, who had been reading along from the card in his hand.

"What's the charge?" Sam asked, his public face not wavering.

"The murder of Wanda Borowski, for a start," Fred said. "And after tonight, I'm pretty sure we can add the murder of George Petris and the attempted murder of Elmer Rush."

Joan didn't hear the assorted gasps and murmurings around them. She was watching Elmer's face crumple. His head kept nodding and tears rolled down the criss-crossed lines of his cheeks. For the first time, she saw him as really old. She was relieved to see the second bassoonist lean toward him and take his hand.

In contrast, Evelyn Wade was becoming more childish by the moment. Sam addressed her as he might a very little girl.

"Now, Evelyn, I want you to do something for me. I'll need a lawyer."

"You *are* a lawyer!" Her voice was petulant.

"I know, but that won't help. Get Burton." With the pencil on his music stand, he scribbled a message on the back of an envelope pulled from his jacket pocket. "Give him this note."

"I don't think so," Fred said quietly. "I'll take that, Sam. You know how we do it."

To Joan's amazement, he plucked the envelope from Sam's hand by a corner and laid it on a white handkerchief that Sergeant Ketcham produced from thin air.

Backing away from Evelyn and Sam, Fred lifted the flap of the envelope with a pencil point and peered inside.

"Looks like the stuff, Johnny," he said. "That and the knife should settle it." He let the flap close and put the handkerchief-wrapped envelope into his pocket.

Sam Wade sat utterly still.

"Come on, sir," said Ketcham. "Let's go."

Sam stood obediently, avoiding all eyes. Evelyn was staring at him, her mouth agape.

"Tell them it's not true, Sam!"

Sam was silent.

"My God, I can't believe it! You couldn't have been so stupid." Angry tears glistened in her eyes.

"Just call the lawyer, Evelyn," he said.

Chin high, she exited upstage left.

# Chapter Twenty-Seven

Henry Skomp and Yoichi Nakamura arrived at the center almost simultaneously five minutes before closing time. Joan welcomed Henry gratefully; the board hadn't yet come to a decision on the subject of after-five adult day care. In theory, it didn't exist. In fact, she was still it.

Her chance to rest disappeared, however, when Yoichi asked her to help call an extra rehearsal to replace the one that had fallen apart the night before.

"Alex is worried about the Schubert and we have not yet read through the rest of the program. We have only three more weeks."

"What will we do for oboes?"

"For this concert, I think we must hire them. I am working on it with Alex. She is talking to the IU Music School today. Would you please call the section leaders whose names I have checked here? Ask them all to notify the members of their sections and to report to you or me if someone cannot come."

He handed her a list of players. Neat brush strokes eliminated the names George Petris, Gideon Samuel Wade, and Wanda Borowski.

Later, at home, Joan kicked off her shoes, padded to the refrigerator for ice cubes and orange juice, and started down the list.

Except for having witnessed Sam's arrest, the section leaders were little different from the people at the center who had played "Isn't it awful?" all day. To most, she said honestly, "I haven't heard any more than you already know."

Only the bare facts had made it into the *Courier*. Sam wasn't talking and Elmer's daughter had refused to let the reporter interview him.

Nancy was another story.

"Didn't I tell you?" she said. "Evelyn never cared two hoots about Sam. You know what she did this morning, of course."

"No, but I imagine you'll tell me."

"I got it from Hazel Baines, who works at the bank. Evelyn marched in there at nine sharp, cool as a cucumber, and cleaned out their joint accounts. She even brought in the key to the safe-deposit box, but of course Hazel couldn't see what she did there. It's all over town. Gil Snarr told his wife that Evelyn dropped by the funeral home and asked him to sell their double plot. She's pulled the kids out of school and Jim Hendricks says he's supposed to bring a van for her furniture tomorrow. It looks as though she isn't leaving a thing behind that isn't nailed down. Sam can't stop her. They won't let him out on bail."

"Poor Sam," Joan said.

"Poor Sam! Joan, he murdered two people!"

"Did he?"

"Well, of course he did. They don't go around arresting the county prosecutor unless they have an airtight case."

Not even a change of venue would affect that point of view, Joan thought. She wondered what Fred had turned up to change his mind and just how airtight his case against Sam was. He had sounded pretty sure of himself at the rehearsal, especially after he opened the envelope.

She was relieved when the doorbell broke into the conversation. "Gotta go, Nancy. There's someone at the door. Don't forget to call the trombones."

Fred stood on her doorstep, neither downcast nor wearing the cocky grin of the night before. She discovered that she was ridiculously pleased to see him.

"Come in, come in. I only have about a million questions to ask you."

"You and everyone else." But he smiled and settled into the one big chair in the little house.

"Would you like something to drink? Orange juice on the rocks?"

"You wouldn't have a cup of coffee, would you?"

"Sure." She started the pot and set out a couple of mugs. When she returned to the living room, she found Andrew and Fred head to head.

"What did I miss?"

"He wouldn't tell me anything, Mom," Andrew complained. "He said we had to wait for you."

"You deserve to hear it all," Fred said. "If it hadn't been for you, we might never have figured it out."

"Me?" The grin spreading across her face felt foolish even from behind. She was glad she couldn't see it. He grinned back.

"Sure, you. First you sent Yoichi to the police."

"No," she said in horror. "I sent him to Sam. If I hadn't, George would have been the only person to die. You do still think Wanda died because...because Sam was afraid of something she might say?"

"Probably," he said gently. "Especially if he told her Daniel wanted him to pick up the oboe, and she already knew that Daniel was on his way over to do it himself. But Sam wouldn't have stopped with George. And it didn't make any difference that he heard it first. He had access to all the police reports anyway. It was good we found out when we did. The first murder was so near to a perfect crime that we wouldn't have caught it if Yoichi hadn't told us about the poison. And then, when you found the reeds, you saw how easy it would be to poison an oboe player with something like TTX. If we'd identified the poison in the reeds sooner, we'd have asked Wanda where the oboe was. And that would have led us straight to Sam if she'd been alive to tell it."

"I should have found them sooner."

The bottle had been right there the whole time she had fought *Donna Diana*. Now the viola line pounded through her head in maddening perfection, as she had never yet been able to play it. She sank to the sofa, resisting with difficulty the feeling that if she covered her ears, everything would be all right again.

"You didn't," Fred said. "I wish I didn't know how you feel. It happens."

She nodded, unable to speak.

"But you did figure out what killed her, you know."

"The reed knife? Was it really?" She found it scant comfort.

"Not the one you thought. Sam used his own. When I asked him to show me what one looked like, he pulled it out of his pocket. Seems it didn't fit in his case and so he carried it in his pants most of the time. It's a handy blade and sturdy. He couldn't very well say no when I borrowed it to ask Dr. Henshaw whether George's reed knife could have been the weapon used on Wanda. I didn't happen to mention to Henshaw whose knife it was.

"On Tuesday he reported to me that he'd found blood of Wanda's type inside the handle. There's quite a good-sized opening on either side of the blade where it fits into the handle."

"So that's what made you think Wade did it?" Andrew asked.

"No, as a matter of fact, by the time I heard that, I was already sure. It will come in mighty handy in court, though."

"What did, then?"

"Well, son, your mother came to see me the other night to show me a bottle of reeds she'd found. Several oboe reeds and one big bassoon reed, all soaking in what looked like plain water. I came up with the theory that Elmer Rush, the man who played bassoon behind Petris, had killed him.

"First thing, I went to Professor Werner's laboratory to make sure the liquid in the bottle was full of his poison. To make a long story short, it was. And Rush had the opportunity to poison the bottle when he and Petris were making reeds. So did Petris, of course, but we knew by that time we were dealing with murder, not suicide. My theory was that Rush had recognized Petris from about twenty years ago, as the lifeguard who let his granddaughter almost drown. She's been in bad shape ever since."

"Why would he wait until now?" Andrew asked.

"Good question. I didn't ask it. About that time I wasn't thinking too clearly. Wade had persuaded my chief of detectives that I was wasting valuable departmental time and making a general fool of myself. I had orders to stick to my knitting and forget about the Petris business. It was supposed to be a figment of Yoichi Nakamura's imagination." He shook his head.

"I was about ready to forget about police business altogether. Now I know he was trying to make sure no one investigated that murder too carefully. He succeeded. I spun my wheels a lot." He shook his head again, slowly. "I just didn't care anymore."

"I was worried about you, Fred," Joan said. "What changed? I hardly knew you last night."

"What changed was that I found out who the lifeguard really was and I knew I'd been had."

"Sam?" asked Joan. "Not George?"

"Sam."

"How did you find out?"

"Martha Lambert, Elmer's daughter, didn't know him as Sam, but she hadn't forgotten his name. She said the lifeguard was a kid from the Bible Belt by the name of Gideon. She didn't think she'd ever forget that. It took her a while to remember the Wade part. Wade—from Fish Creek—that's how she remembered. She didn't know how close that was to Oliver. Never crossed her mind when they moved here."

"Nancy told me they called him Giddy before he left home. He went out west to train for the Olympic swim team."

"That's right. The only people back here who knew what had happened were his parents. They went out to California to see him through and take custody of him. Then they made him enlist in the marines. Mrs. Lambert knew that much. That's the last she remembered hearing about him."

"You said Wanda's killer probably had military training," Joan reminded him.

"Did I?"

"Mmm. Fred, how come this made you sure Sam was the killer? You'd already figured out that Elmer had recognized the lifeguard."

His blue eyes laughed.

"This was different. If Elmer had meant to kill Sam, then he wouldn't have poisoned George's reed bottle."

"If all this was between Elmer and Sam, then how did George get into it at all?" Joan was lost.

"Maybe partly because you fell down. I didn't know about that until last night, but I suspected something of the sort. Look, I had it all backwards. Elmer didn't recognize Sam. I've seen pictures of Sam in college and law school. You'd need a lot of imagination to pick that fellow out of a crowd today. He doesn't have any physical peculiarities. This year he doesn't even have a suntan. His hair is going gray and it's brushed back over his ears. Elmer would remember a kid in a crew cut."

"I get it!" Andrew fairly shouted. "It was the old guy who didn't change. You know, Mom, how much Grandpa looks like the pictures of him with me when I was little? But I've changed a lot."

"That's it, Andrew," said Fred. "Sam Wade recognized Elmer Rush, not the other way around."

"But why would Wade want revenge?" Andrew asked. "It didn't mess his life up all that much."

"Oh," said Joan, seeing Evelyn's face clearly. "He didn't. All Sam wanted was his wife, and all she wanted was a political career—second-hand, through him. If the word had leaked out about his criminal youth, she'd have thrown him over about as fast as I gather she has. He wasn't just careless, Andrew. He was drinking on the job and underage, too. Julie nearly died. As it is, she'll probably never tie her own shoes, much less read a book. He had to hide it."

"You'd think someone would have found out by now," Andrew said.

"His parents died before he went into politics," Fred said. "The legal records are sealed because of his age at the time. They may even have been purged by now. It wasn't likely to come up."

"Oh, but it was," said Joan. "Nancy told me Evelyn made him use all three names when he campaigned. That's how it was on the orchestra list, too. Elmer would have spotted Gideon Samuel Wade. The only reason we didn't hand those lists out a week ago was that George died and shook us up."

"I'm guessing that he managed to forget the whole sorry episode until he saw Julie's grandfather in the orchestra," Fred said. "And I'm not sure that Sam was quite as ambitious as Evelyn. He could probably have been elected to Congress with no problem on that score—and reelected, if the local folks liked him."

"What was that about Mom falling down?" Andrew asked.

"Now I'm really speculating," Fred answered. "Last night I asked the people to imitate what they did in the last few minutes before George Petris collapsed. I was hoping that Sam would make one last attempt on Elmer Rush and that, because we were expecting it, we'd be able to keep it from happening and catch him in the act. That's pretty much how it turned out.

"He came prepared with an ordinary white envelope. In one corner, nearly invisible, there was enough TTX to kill off most of the woodwinds. Probably from Werner's lab, though there's no way to tell. I don't know if he would have tried using it with me there, but when I offered him what looked like George's bottle of reeds, he passed it right back to Elmer and pointed out the one bassoon reed in it. When we stopped that and called him on it, he tried to get rid of the envelope of TTX by passing it to his wife with a note on it. Now we have that, too."

"You were going to tell me about how Mom fell," Andrew reminded him.

"Sort of," Joan said. "I faked it."

"She knocked over the plastic cup Elmer was using last night to soak his reeds," Fred said. "Last week, the thing she knocked over when she fell was the prescription bottle she took home after the rehearsal. A bassoon reed hid the oboe reeds in it. When she picked things up after she fell, she saw the bassoon reed in it and put it back by Elmer's chair."

"That could be," Joan said slowly. "There was a lid on it, and I couldn't see inside all that well. I didn't even read the label with George's name on it until I found it at home, much later. I was rushing, because he was yelling at me for falling all over his music stand."

Does that make it my fault or his that he was killed? she wondered.

"That was the bottle Sam poisoned," Fred said. "He was after Elmer, not George. But George found his reeds in the wrong place and took one out to use. He died because Sam didn't see the oboe reeds when he dropped the TTX into the bottle."

"That seems odd," Joan said. "Sam sat right there all through the break. Why would he wait until we all came back to do what he could have done while no one was around? I'll bet he'd already poisoned the reeds by then. After all, the bottle must have been back near Elmer while they were working on the reeds, if he put his bassoon reed into it."

She felt better.

"Maybe," Fred said. "Either way, Sam was trying to kill Elmer, not the other way around." He didn't seem threatened by her arguing. "And he had to do it before Elmer saw his name on that personnel list."

"Seems to me you should have known all along that Mr. Rush didn't do it," Andrew said.

"How's that?" Fred asked.

"I don't see how he'd know about the poison. They say everybody in town knew it, but Mom and I didn't. We weren't here last spring when the newspaper ran that big feature about the lab. Wasn't he new in town, too?"

Joan hugged him. "Andrew, I wish I had let you in on this the other night. I would have spared myself a lot of grief. I couldn't bear to think that Elmer had killed someone."

He wouldn't have, she thought. And I wouldn't have. Humming, she got up to pour the coffee.

"I wonder what would have happened if the first murder had turned out the way it was supposed to," Andrew mused.

"Do you think Wade would have gone after the rest of the family?"

"I'm sure he thought they were still in California," said Fred. "The kids didn't know about him at all—but how could he be sure of that? You might be right, Andrew."

"We still don't know what happened to George's oboe—or his reed knife," said Joan.

"Didn't I tell you? The janitor picked up his knife the next day, figured some kid had brought it to school, and gave it to the principal." Fred shook his head. "Something in this morning's paper finally made him think it over again and call us."

"And the oboe?"

"It's gone. I imagine Sam dumped it in some abandoned quarry. He could have carried it anywhere, for that matter, and no one would have thought a thing about it. It looked just like his. I don't think we'll ever know for sure, unless he decides to confess."

"Do you think that's likely?" Joan thought Sam might have very little reason to hold back now.

"Not really. It will all depend on his lawyer. Sam doesn't seem to be making any decisions on his own. I don't think he cares."

He took a sip of his coffee and sat staring into the mug.

"It's hard to believe that just last week he had me completely buffaloed. He raked me and young Pruitt over the coals for having the gall to question his secretary about his movements on Saturday. I believed him for a long time, too. It seemed that he could have had less than ten minutes to arrive, kill Wanda, clean up, and walk back to the office.

"Then you figured out that he could have killed her before starting the washer, but the times were still too tight. For a while, I thought Evelyn Wade did it. Miss Hobbs said a light blue Seville drove past at about the right time. That's her car."

"Oh, no," Joan said. "Evelyn spent the whole day on foot, shoe shopping. I'm sure the clerks all over town could give you a shoe-by-shoe account. She had to walk because Sam's car was in the shop. That means he was using hers."

"You mean he drove," Andrew said. "That's how he got there and back so fast."

"You two," Fred said. "We could use you both."

"You're doing the hiring these days?" Joan asked.

"Not quite, but my stock has gone up a little. Not that that's saying much, when you realize that Sam asked for me on the Petris case. He must have thought, 'Now which man can I trust not to get it right?' That's what really lit a fire under me when I heard Martha Lambert say his name."

"Oh, Fred."

"Don't 'oh, Fred' me. Captain Altschuler patted me on the back and made a little speech today. I'll know he means it if I move up from bicycles and lost dogs to stolen cars and missing persons. Next year's an election year. I can wait."

They sat in comfortable silence. Joan refilled the mugs.

"Fred," she said after a while. "I still have one question."

"What's that?"

"Could you really have played the oboe solo on that sax?"

Printed in the United States
2413